CHAPTER 1

Murder was rarely random, despite what the media peddled for ratings. It was usually personal. Intimate even. Enough so, sometimes, that you could identify the killer from the crime itself. Like a signature.

"The killer knew the victim," posited Larry Chen, detective with the Seattle Police Department. He was tall, barrel-chested, with the years as a homicide detective seemingly weighing on his broad shoulders.

"And hated him," added Dave Brunelle, prosecutor with the King County Prosecutor's Office. He was also tall, but not quite as tall as Chen, and his shoulders, while they had seen almost as much, rested far easier than the detective's.

"Or loved him," Chen suggested, "and it turned."

Brunelle nodded. "It's hard to get that angry at someone," he pointed at the body, "without already having strong emotions for them."

The murder had indeed been intimate, and brutal. In fact, its brutality was part of what made it intimate. It had been up close, and it had taken a while. It was no gunshot across a parking lot.

No gunshot at all. It was a knife. Well, an 'edged weapon' as they said in the cop training. But probably a knife. For one thing, most 'edged weapons' were knives. For another, the wounds were punctures not slices. Brunelle couldn't completely rule out something like a razor or a machete, but he was experienced enough to know the medical examiner would do that for him. The killer, whoever he or she was, had used a knife to stab the victim, repeatedly, and the rips in the clothing were small enough to suggest the knife wasn't up to finishing the task with one blow. Another point for an intimate, emotional, angry murder. The killer had grabbed what was at hand and made do, rather than having brought a better weapon for the job, calculated and cold-blooded.

The number of wounds was telltale as well. It wasn't one to the throat, or to the heart, or even in the back. It looked like half a dozen, frantically dispersed across the victim's torso and face. There was no way to know the order of the strikes, but Brunelle guessed the two to the face may have been first. They must have been unexpected—no one lets their face get stabbed. If the victim had seen the knife coming, those would have ended up as defensive wounds on his forearms, not a pair of gashes just below his left eye.

It would also have stunned the victim enough, Brunelle opined, to allow the killer to follow up with all of the other small stab wounds tracking downward until the tip of the handy, but ill-suited blade finally nicked the outer edge of the victim's heart.

Brunelle considered for a moment.

Or the killer got lucky on the first stab, pierced the victim's heart, and followed with a frenzy upward toward the face they knew and, at least in that moment, hated.

Either way, the victim was dead. It was Chen's job to find his killer. And it would be Brunelle's job to send him to prison for the rest of his life.

"Any leads?" Brunelle asked. He couldn't start his job until Chen finished his. He wondered how long the wait might be.

"Not yet," Chen admitted, "but we just got here. We're about to go talk to the neighbor who called 9-1-1. You want to observe?"

Brunelle scanned the scene again. Dead guy in the middle of the living room, face up on a carpet stained with his own blood. Freshly dead, but not too fresh. The blood was starting to dry into a sticky black paste. He was late 20s to early 30s, white, with a fresh haircut and neatly trimmed beard. No obvious signs of a struggle, apart from the dead body. All of the expensive looking furnishings were in order, including some sort of multi-computer cluster in the corner that Brunelle knew he wouldn't understand and also probably cost more than his car.

The apartment itself was a typical two-bedroom unit in Seattle's South Lake Union District, the new trendy neighborhood recently filled in with young tech workers and the eclectic restaurants and clubs that catered to young professionals with no kids and too much money. Brunelle wasn't young anymore and he definitely didn't have too much money after a career in public service. He remembered when that area was the warehouses between the freeway and Seattle Center, home of the Space Needle and the old Coliseum where the NBA's SuperSonics played before being bought and moved by a bunch of out-of-towners with way too much money. Back then, the only thing that area was known for was the terrible traffic planning for what should have obviously been a major thoroughfare, but ended up in a snarl of traffic known unaffectionately as the 'Mercer Mess', named after the street everyone was stuck on for hours after every one of those Sonics games.

Mercer Street was named after Asa Mercer, a man who earned his place in Seattle history by making a pilgrimage to Chicago in the late 1800s and returning to the Emerald City with a large number of women to marry the men in the overwhelmingly male frontier town of Seattle. It made him a legend. They even made a campy T.V. series about it back in the '60s. For his heroics, he got a street, an arena, and even an entire island named after him.

If it had been fifty years earlier, the apartment building they were standing in would have been named the Mercer Arms. Twenty-five years earlier, it would have been the Mercer Lofts. But right then, the neighborhood filled with rich techies was also filled with apartment complexes named after whatever their street address happened to be. So instead of finding themselves in the Mercer Apartments or Mercer Gardens or even just The Mercer, they were inside 'The Six-12'. Brunelle tried not to roll his eyes at the thought of it all. An eye roll was just proof that he was getting old. And no one cared what an old guy like him thought anyway.

"Sure," he answered Chen's invitation to observe the witness interview.

"Great," Chen answered. "I'd like to know what you think."

No one but other old guys like him.

CHAPTER 2

Ramona Gray seemed to fit the demographic for The Six-12. Late twenty-something, dark complexion and hair, with stylish clothes and hairstyle that suggested she had recently moved to Seattle from somewhere else and hadn't yet given in to the native garb of dark sportswear and daily ponytails. She was also in tech, judging by a computer array even more impressive than her dead neighbor's, and a variety of jackets and messenger bags by her front door all emblazoned with the logo for some tech company Brunelle had never heard of but had no doubt was paying multiple times his salary, plus stock options.

But the fat bank account and fancy clothes were no protection against the horror of losing a neighbor, and possibly friend, to senseless violence. She was seated on her custom couch, a patrol officer standing guard at a respectable distance, as they awaited the arrival of the lead detective. And his Prosecutor Friday.

"Ms. Gray," Chen stepped up to her and extended a hand. "I'm Detective Chen. I have a few questions for you, if you're up to it."

Gray stared up at the detective with large, dark-rimmed eyes. She nodded. "Of course." Brunelle had expected her voice to break, but despite her generally distraught facial expression, her voice was steady. She nodded at Brunelle. "Who's he?"

"He's my assistant," Chen answered before Brunelle could even part his lips. "He's just here to observe."

Brunelle kept those lips unparted, but they twisted into a perturbed knot.

"You were friends with Mr. Rycroft?" Chen began.

"Charlie? Yeah," Gray confirmed. "Sort of. I mean, I don't know about friends, exactly. More like acquaintances. Neighbors, I guess. We'd stop and talk in the hall sometimes, if we both got home at the same time or something, but we didn't hang out or anything."

"Not dating?" Chen wanted to confirm.

Gray frowned at the suggestion. "Um, no," she assured. "He was not my type."

Brunelle scanned her apartment again. They seemed like the same type.

"So, how did you come to be the one who discovered his body?" Chen asked. "You're the one who called 9-1-1, right?"

Gray nodded. "Right."

"Did you hear an argument or a struggle?" Chen suggested.

But Gray shook her head. "No, nothing like that. I mean, I don't think so. I just heard a normal, 'someone's in the apartment next door' sound and figured he was home again. He'd been gone on vacation or something, I guess."

"How would you know that if you were only neighbors?" Chen questioned.

"Because I got a package of his delivered to my mailbox downstairs last week," Gray explained. "I'd been trying to give it to him for a few days, but he never answered."

"Did you try calling him?" Chen asked.

"Like, on the telephone?" Gray scoffed. "Um, no. But I texted and snapped him, but he left me on read."

Brunelle squinted at the response, waiting for his brain to be able to understand it, but with only partial success. It didn't help him feel any younger.

"Okay," Chen didn't seem to fully grasp it either. He moved on. "Did you ever just go over and knock on his door?"

"For sure, after a couple of days," Gray answered, "but he was never there when I knocked. I mean, I could have just returned it to sender, or whatever, but that would have been kind of a bitch thing to do, right? So, I was just waiting to run into him, but after he didn't answer his door for a few days, I figured he was out of town. I tried one last time tonight when I got home from work, but there was still no answer, so I figured I was done."

"What time was that?" Chen asked.

Gray thought for a moment. "Around eight, I think. Then a couple of hours later, I heard somebody in there, so I thought I'd give it one more try."

"So, you knocked on the door again?" Chen surmised.

"Yes," Gray confirmed.

"Did you see anyone coming or going from the apartment," Chen asked. "Anyone in the hallway or anything?"

Gray shrugged. "I definitely didn't see anyone coming out of the apartment. Could there have been someone down at the end of the hallway? Maybe. I wasn't really looking. I mean, I didn't know it would be important."

But it was important, Brunelle knew. Or it would have been, if she'd seen someone and could have offered at least a partial description of the suspect.

"Of course not," Chen soothed. "Just thought I'd ask, in case you did see someone. So, how did you get into the apartment? Was the door ajar?"

When is a door not a door? Brunelle thought that to himself every time he heard the word 'ajar'. Every time. It was sort of annoying actually.

"No." Gray frowned and looked away. "I tried the handle," she admitted. "It was unlocked."

"So, you just went inside?" Chen asked.

"I was really sick of having that package," Gray defended. "It had been days of having this obligation sitting on my table every time I came or went from my apartment. Honestly, I was about to send it back after all. So, when I heard someone next door, I decided I'd try one more time, and if he still wasn't home, then I'd write 'Return to Sender' on it and leave it down by the mailboxes."

"So, you entered his apartment without permission," Chen confirmed.

"He didn't answer when I knocked," Gray answered, "but I knew I'd heard something. I thought maybe he was gaming with headphones on or doing something else where he couldn't hear me knock."

Like being dead on the floor, Brunelle supposed.

"So, the door was closed, but unlocked," Chen clarified.

"Yes."

"Did you close the door behind you when you came inside?"

Brunelle frowned. He knew where Chen was going with

that. And he knew where it would end up.

"I mean, it just sort of closed behind me automatically," Gray explained.

"Which means," Chen followed up, "when you left, you had to grab the inside door handle and twist it to open the door again?"

"Yes. Why?" Gray asked. Then her eyebrows shot up. "Oh. Fingerprints, right?"

"Not anymore," Brunelle muttered. Both Gray and Chen glanced over at the interruption. "Sorry. Carry on."

"What did you see when you came inside?" Chen returned to his questioning.

Gray shrugged and gestured toward her own floor. "Him. Charlie. On the floor. Dead."

"He was already dead when you got inside?" Chen asked.

"I mean, I think so," Gray answered. "I didn't check to be sure, like take a pulse or anything. I didn't want to touch anything."

"Except the door handles," Brunelle muttered again.

"But you didn't see any signs of life?" Chen either didn't hear Brunelle or decided to ignore him.

"He wasn't moving," Gray answered. "His eyes were open but just looked, well, dead. There was blood all over his chest and all over the carpet. I'm pretty sure he was dead."

"So, what did you do?"

"I ran out and back to my apartment. I locked my door. And then I called 9-1-1."

"Did you see anyone else in Charlie's apartment?"

Gray shook her head. "No, but I guess there could have been someone in the bedroom or something. I don't know.

That's why I locked my door, I guess. I just got out of there as fast as I could. I didn't even leave the stupid package there. It was still in my hand when I ran out."

"And you waited in your apartment until the police arrived?" Chen asked.

"Yes, absolutely."

"Did you see or hear anything else from Charlie's apartment that you haven't already told us?"

Gray took a moment to think. "No. That's everything. I don't know what happened or why or who did it. I just called 9-1-1 and waited for you guys to show up."

Chen nodded several times, his lips twisted into a thoughtful knot. Then he looked over to Brunelle. "Do you have any questions?"

Brunelle was pleased to be asked. He took a step forward.

"As a matter of fact, I do." He nodded toward the cardboard box Ramona Gray had dropped on her dining room table. "What's in the package?"

CHAPTER 3

"A bottle of Canadian Mist?" laughed Brunelle's girlfriend, Casey Emory, detective with the suburban Bellevue Police Department, that night over dinner. "That's what was in the package? What even is that?"

"It's blended whiskey, I think," Brunelle answered. "I'd have to go to the liquor store to be sure."

"Or google it," Emory suggested.

"Or google it," Brunelle confirmed with a pained smile.

"Yep," Emory looked up from her phone. "Blended whiskey from Ontario, bottled at forty percent alcohol. Generally considered uncomplex and inexpensive."

"Uncomplex and inexpensive," Brunelle repeated. "Weird gift."

"Weirder name," Emory said.

Brunelle cocked his head. "Why?"

"Well, I mean, if you speak German," Emory expounded. "Which, as we know all too well, you do not."

Brunelle crossed his arms. "I did okay."

"Yes, you did," Emory consoled with a pout, "Davey."

Brunelle shook his head and unfolded his arms. "Whatever. Why is it weird in German or whatever?"

Emory laughed again. "Because 'Mist' is the German word for manure. Canadian manure doesn't sound like anything I'd like to drink."

"I wonder if they export to Germany?" Brunelle pondered.

"I doubt it," Emory said, "but I could google it."

"Please don't." Brunelle raised a hand.

"Do you want to know what the word 'Gift' means in German?" Emory offered.

"Not today," Brunelle answered. "The point is, the package was a dead end. Larry's out trying to round up some possible suspects. I don't think the murder was random. It happened inside his apartment, and there were no signs of forced entry. It was someone he knew, so Larry's gonna start figuring out who he knew, and where they were when he was killed."

"A sound investigative approach," Emory approved, "but keep an eye on that neighbor. She's either your only witness, or there are no witnesses to contradict her claim."

Brunelle considered for a moment. "Or both."

"Yeah, or both," Emory agreed. "Probably both."

"Probably both," Brunelle agreed.

"So, what do you do now, Mr. Prosecutor?" Emory asked. "You can't prosecute anyone until there's a person to prosecute."

"No, but I can still prepare," Brunelle replied.

"How?"

"I may not know who the killer is yet," Brunelle explained. "But I know who the victim is. I'm going to the autopsy tomorrow morning."

CHAPTER 4

There was nothing quite like the smell of a fresh autopsy first thing in the morning. Actually, the smell wouldn't be that bad. The body wasn't really decomposed. They'd found the body relatively fresh and it had spent the night in a refrigerated room at the King County Medical Examiner's Office. Also, Brunelle was allowed to step back and hold a cup of coffee up to his face as the Assistant Medical Examiner proceeded with the examination. It wasn't like they needed to worry about the risk of infection.

"You sure you want to be out here in the examining room?" asked Dr. Jack Tockle, the pathologist who was about to carve open Charlie Rycroft's body. He was older than Brunelle, an increasingly rare thing, with a smoker's voice and a mop of white hair on top of his pudgy, clean-shaven face. He nodded toward a door on the other side of the room. "We have a perfectly good observation room over there."

"I know." Brunelle had watched other autopsies from that room. "I want to watch this one close up. I'm curious about the wounds, what type of weapon was used, stuff like that."

"You know I write a report when I'm done, right?" Tockle frowned at him.

"You know I already have too much to read, right?" Brunelle returned.

Tockle shrugged. "Suit yourself. I doubt you'll gain anything from hovering over my shoulder, but at least I'll find it annoying."

"I'm a lawyer," Brunelle said. "I'm supposed to be annoying."

"Your words, not mine," Tockle muttered. Then he threw back the sheet covering Rycroft's naked corpse. "You ready to begin?"

"Sure," Brunelle answered. "Can we start with time of death? Can you confirm it was at ten-thirty last night?"

Tockle frowned at him. "I thought you were more experienced than that. You know I can't pinpoint an exact time. Not that exact anyway. Within a few hours, maybe. But I can confirm that he was almost certainly dead at the time my technicians put him into a body bag."

"Great," Brunelle said sarcastically. "Very helpful."

"Glad I could help," Tockle replied. "Now, let's see what we have here."

What they had there was pretty obvious, at least on the larger scale. Tockle dictated it into a recorder he balanced on the edge of the examining table. "Caucasian male. Appearance consistent with reported age of thirty-one years old. Multiple sharp force wounds to the anterior torso, neck, and head. No other obvious signs of injury."

Brunelle took a sip of his coffee. So far, his untrained observations matched up with the guy with the medical degree.

It was the next bit that was going to prove informative. Or so Brunelle hoped, anyway.

"Will now examine the wounds in order, from superior to inferior."

Head to toe, Brunelle translated silently. He'd spent a career translating expert jargon and cop slang to juries. He did it without thinking anymore.

"The superior-most injury is a penetrative incised wound, approximately two centimeters in length, located approximately three centimeters inferior to the left orbital socket."

Small stab wound, about an inch below the left eye.

"Observable tearing of the skin at the edges of the wound."

Dull knife.

"The next injury is lateral to the superior injury and approximately five centimeters inferior, presenting the same approximate length and irregular edge."

Low and outside, same small dull knife.

Brunelle was wondering whether he might duck into the observation room after all. He'd forgotten how cold they kept those examining rooms. The coffee was keeping his fingers warm, but his toes were freezing.

"Oh." Tockle paused. "Now, that's surprising."

Or maybe Brunelle could just kick his feet together and stick around a bit longer after all.

"What is?" he asked.

"This next wound is different," Tockle answered. "I'm not sure yet, but I don't think it was made with the same object as the injuries to the face."

Brunelle narrowed his eyes at that suggestion. "The

killer switched knives mid-murder?"

Tockle frowned. "I'm not even sure these were knives, frankly. They were sharp enough to break the skin, but they're irregularly shaped. I'll know more when we start to peel away the layers and I can get a look inside of the wounds, but this isn't your everyday kitchen knife stabbing."

"Everyday?" Brunelle questioned.

Tockle sighed. "I guess it just seems like it's every day. For me at least. But then something like this pops up to keep things interesting. I guess that's why I haven't retired yet. Well, that and I want to squeeze every last penny out of that pension I've got coming."

Brunelle raised his cup to that. Finally, something good about getting older. Another day closer to retirement and his government pension. He ignored the fact that he probably could have made so much more in private practice that his IRA would have outperformed any pension.

Tockle leaned over the body and quickly scanned each of the remaining wounds. He stood upright again, shaking his head. "I can't say for sure yet, but we might be dealing with three or even four different weapons here, counselor. This is going to take a while. I'm going to need to be very careful as I work my way down on those wounds. You should rethink that observation room."

Brunelle already had. He couldn't feel his toes despite kicking them against the floor.

"Sounds good, doc. Let me know what you find out. Those wounds have got me curious."

Tockle nodded and looked back at the corpse. "Me too."

* * *

"You are not going to believe it," Tockle said when he

entered the observation room hours later. "I hardly believe it."

"What?" Brunelle looked up from his phone. He hadn't thought to bring his work laptop with him, so he had tried to sign in remotely from his phone like he was supposed to be able to do, but he hadn't really paid attention at the training, and it was definitely not intuitive. Eventually he had given up. But he had managed to clear a few dozen levels of Candy Crush, so the wait wasn't a complete waste of time.

"There are eight wounds total," Tockle explained. "Every one of them is a stab wound. But there were five different weapons."

"Five?" That was hard to believe.

"Yep," the doctor confirmed. "And do you want to know what's even stranger?"

"Yes," Brunelle answered. "Of course."

"I think only one of them was actually a knife," Tockle said. "Like an actual fixed blade designed to cut and penetrate a human body."

"I'm not sure all knives are designed to stab people," Brunelle couldn't stop himself from pointing out. Lawyers, annoying.

"You know what I mean," Tockle grumbled. "Only one of them was a knife blade. The rest were sharp enough to do the job, but only with a lot of force, and they left a path that made it clear they were designed for something other than stabbing people."

Brunelle stopped himself from reiterating his previous point. "So, what were they?"

Tockle frowned. "You a fisherman?"

"A fisherman? No," Brunelle replied. "I mean, I went a few times with my dad when I was a kid, but it was never really—Wait, did he get stabbed with a fishing hook?"

"No, a fish scaler," Tockle answered.

"A fish scaler?" Brunelle asked. "What's that?"

"Did you have a Swiss Army knife as a kid?" Tockle asked.

"Sure," Brunelle said. "Everyone did."

"You remember that weird long thing, with two prongs at the end and a serrated edge on one side?" Tockle asked. "Sometimes they even marked it with a ruler on the smooth edge."

Brunelle shook his head. "I don't recall that. But then again—"

"You weren't a fisherman," Tockle finished his thought. "Well, I'm pretty sure that's what got plunged into his face twice. I wasn't sure until I saw the ones on his chest. I'm pretty sure one of those is from a corkscrew and another is from that combination screwdriver-bottle cap opener thing."

Brunelle blinked at the medical examiner. "He was killed by a Swiss Army knife?"

Tockle nodded. "Well, sort of. The one to the neck? That was the knife blade. Clean incision, clear through his carotid artery. That's what killed him. The others? I don't know. They could have been fatal if untreated, but it was the one to the neck that took him out."

"So, the killer kept changing tools on the Swiss Army knife and plunging it back into the victim's body?" Brunelle was having trouble believing that, which meant the jury would too. He needed to be certain before he took that theory to trial.

"I'm pretty sure that's right." Tockle shrugged. "Like some crazy *Murder on the Orient Express*, except it was one murderer and he was a boy scout."

Brunelle didn't say anything because he didn't know what that meant.

"I want to do some more tests though," Tockle continued. "I haven't seen a lot of injuries caused by the lesser-used tools of a Swiss Army knife. I probably wouldn't even have thought of it if there hadn't been so many different patterns of tearing. I think I'm going to get some pig flesh and a Swiss Army knife and see if I can reproduce the injuries." He chuckled. "I'm gonna need to buy a new Swiss Army knife, though. I haven't had one of those since I was a kid."

"No one has," Brunelle replied. Which was good. It would narrow down the possible suspects, although he doubted Charlie Rycroft was murdered by a rogue boy scout. Maybe he hadn't paid for his girl scout cookie order. In any event, Brunelle needed to let Chen know as soon as possible. Tockle's report wouldn't be complete for several days if he was going to have to go Swiss Army knife shopping first.

Brunelle pulled out his phone and called the detective.

"Chen," he answered.

"Larry? It's Brunelle. We've had a development in the Rycroft case. What are you doing right now?"

"I'm at P.N.W. Outfitters."

That was a weird coincidence. "Are you going camping? I might need you to pick up something for Doc Tockle."

"What? No," Chen answered. "I'm contacting Rycroft's next of kin. His parents are both dead, but he has a brother who works at the P.N.W. flagship store in South Lake Union. In fact, it's only a couple of blocks from our dead guy's apartment."

"Don't do anything," Brunelle said. "I'll be there in fifteen minutes. I'll meet you in the outdoor tool and equipment section."

"Where?"

"Swiss Army knives," Brunelle clarified. "You're not going to believe this."

CHAPTER 5

"A Swiss Army knife?" Chen stared at Brunelle. "Are you fucking kidding me?"

"Whoa, language, Detective Chen," Brunelle laughed. "I'm the one with the potty mouth. But yeah. At least, that's what the medical examiner thinks. He's gonna test it out on some dead pigs."

"He's going to stab a dead pig with a Swiss Army knife?"

Brunelle shrugged. "I know. Seems creepy, right? But you've gotta be a little creepy already to want to be a medical examiner."

Chen nodded at that. "So, what? One of these?" He pointed at the wall display of camping multi-tools. "I mean, was it actually Swiss Army brand? Do they even still make those? Man, I almost cut my thumb off with one of those when I was a kid."

"I don't know what brand it was," Brunelle answered. "I just know it had a corkscrew, a fish scaler, a combo screwdriver-bottle cap opener, and, oh yeah, a knife blade."

"Seems like that last one would be sufficient," Chen remarked.

"If you just wanted to kill him, sure," Brunelle agreed. "That means it's just more evidence that whoever did this had a lot of strong emotions for the victim."

"And a Swiss Army knife," Chen added.

"And a Swiss Army knife," Brunelle agreed.

"Hello there, gentlemen." A salesman walked up and greeted them. He looked a lot like Charlie Rycroft, with the same haircut, but a little shorter and no beard. And no fish scaler puncture wounds to his face. "Can I help you find something?"

Chen pulled out his badge. "We're here to speak with Matthew Rycroft."

The salesman's eyes flashed wide. "I—I'm Matt Rycroft."

"We need to talk to you about your brother Charlie," Chen explained.

"And we might need to buy a Swiss Army knife," Brunelle added with a jerk of his thumb toward the display wall.

"I don't understand," Matt said. "Is Charlie in trouble? Am I in trouble?"

Yes, thought Brunelle, *and maybe.*

"Do you have someplace private we can talk, Mr. Rycroft?" Chen suggested. "Perhaps the room where you detain shoplifters?"

Matt's eyes widened again. "This is a big deal, isn't it?"

"Yes, Mr. Rycroft," Chen answered. "This is a big deal. Now, about that private room?"

* * *

The private room was bigger than Brunelle had

expected, with plenty of room for all three of them. It was, in fact, where P.N.W. detained shoplifters while they waited for the police to arrive with the actual handcuffs and the free ride in a police car. As such, it was undecorated and spartan. It was basically a holding cell without the bars, but there were four chairs—one more than they needed—and a table over which Chen could sit across from Matthew Rycroft.

"I'm sorry to be the bearer of bad news, Mr. Rycroft," Chen began, "but your brother Charlie is dead."

Brunelle and Chen both knew this would only be news if Matt wasn't the killer, in which case, the only real news to him would be that the body had been discovered. And that could hardly be unexpected given the lack of any effort to dispose of the body.

"Dead?" Matt gasped. "Was there an accident?"

Chen shook his head. "He was murdered."

"What?" Matt's eyes flashed again. "Murdered? Oh my God." He put a hand over his mouth. "Does Katie know?"

"Who's Katie?" Chen asked.

"His girlfriend," Matt answered, "and my—" but he stopped himself.

"Your what?" Brunelle encouraged from the sidelines.

"Um, well," Matt shifted in his seat, "my ex-fiancée."

"Your ex-fiancée was dating your brother?" Brunelle followed up, of course.

Matt frowned. "It's a long story."

"I bet," Brunelle grunted.

"When did this happen?" Matt asked. "Who did it? Why? Why would anyone murder Charlie?"

"Those are all the things we're in the process of figuring out, Mr. Rycroft," Chen answered. "That's why we're speaking with you."

"With me?" Matt cocked his head. "I don't understand."

"Where were you Tuesday night between say five in the evening and midnight?" Chen asked.

"Tuesday night?" Matt stammered. "Are you serious? You think I did it?"

"Just answer the question, Mr. Rycroft," Brunelle advised.

"I don't know," Matt answered. "I mean, I'm not sure. I didn't expect—"

"Do you have an alibi, Mr. Rycroft?" Chen asked point-blank.

"I mean, no," Matt answered. "Not right now. But I'll have one by tomorrow."

Chen raised an eyebrow at that, then turned to Brunelle. "Is that enough to charge?"

Brunelle frowned thoughtfully. "Peculiar access to unique murder weapon. Motive of jealousy for losing fiancée to victim. Stated intent to fabricate alibi. I'm not sure it's proof beyond a reasonable doubt, but it sounds like probable cause. It's definitely enough for me to get a seventy-two-hour hold on him while you get a warrant and search his home."

"What?!" Matthew Rycroft wailed, throwing his arms wide.

Chen stood up and pulled the handcuffs off the back of his belt. "Mr. Rycroft, I'm placing you under arrest for the murder of your brother, Charlie Rycroft."

CHAPTER 6

Brunelle was right. It was too thin to convict, but it was enough to arrest and enough for a judge to find probable cause for the arrest. That, in turn, allowed for the continued detention of Matthew Rycroft in the King County Jail while Chen took the time to draft up an affidavit for a search warrant, get it signed by a different judge, and assemble a forensics team to search Rycroft's home across Lake Washington in the suburb of Bellevue, Washington. Brunelle tagged along again, but not to enter the home. If they did find evidence of the murder, he would need to call the person who found it as a witness to explain how and where the item was found. That would be difficult to do if he was the witness himself.

But since the home was outside of Seattle, professional courtesy meant Seattle P.D. teaming up with the local agency to execute the warrant jointly. Local agency meant the Bellevue Police Department. And Bellevue P.D. meant another chance to hang out with his girlfriend.

"What's a nice girl like you doing at a crime scene like this?" he asked as he walked up to Emory and put a hand on her back.

Emory rolled her eyes at him. "Working," she answered. "What's a not-cop like you doing at a cop-thing like this?"

"Just hanging out with my cop-best friend and my cop-girlfriend," Brunelle explained.

"You need to meet more people," Emory suggested.

Brunelle frowned but nodded. "That's probably true. But dating lawyers hasn't worked out for me in the past."

"Maybe a medical examiner?" Emory suggested.

Brunelle winced. "That didn't work out either."

"Well, hopefully this cop thing works out then," Emory said. "Otherwise you may have to start dating defendants."

"Sounds like a conflict of interest," Brunelle replied.

"More than cops, and lawyers, and medical examiners?"

Brunelle forced a grin. "Hey, you know what we should do? We should talk about something else."

"Agreed," Emory chuckled.

"So, where are we?" Brunelle gestured generally at the houses around them. "What neighborhood are we in? Is this Bellevue's Capitol Hill or what?"

Emory laughed again. "Bellevue doesn't have a Capitol Hill."

"That's too bad," Brunelle opined.

"I can agree with that," Emory answered, "but we have plenty of other nice neighborhoods. This one is called Surrey Downs."

"Ooh, sounds fancy," Brunelle enthused.

Emory shrugged. "Meh. It's the first neighborhood south of downtown. Mostly single-family residential, but a lot of rentals. Like your suspect's place." She pointed at the front door of the house where the forensics team was making entry. "This whole town has gotten too expensive for anyone to actually buy anything."

"Even a local city cop?" Brunelle joked.

"Especially a local city cop," Emory answered. She smiled at her boyfriend of increasing duration. "Maybe I need a roommate."

Brunelle knew what that was code for. He wasn't quite ready for the 'moving in together' discussion. Certainly not right then.

"Heh, yeah, anyway." He forced a chuckle, then pointed up at the house too. "So, uh, you're not going in with them?"

Emory shook her head at him, but smiled. "Coward." Then she answered his question. "Nah. I'm just here because it's our city, and because Chen had my number. I can probably thank you for that too, huh?"

"Yes, I will absolutely let you thank me for that," Brunelle joked. "Maybe after dinner tonight?"

Emory shrugged. "Not sure. I'll have to check my schedule. Might need to clean up my solo apartment. By myself."

Brunelle wasn't going to be able to avoid that conversation much longer, he realized.

"Well, let's have that dinner then," he suggested, "and maybe we can talk about these living arrangements of ours."

Emory's eyebrows shot up. "Did you just say that?"

Brunelle struck a thoughtful expression. "I think maybe I did."

"I think you did," Emory laughed.

"I might have," Brunelle agreed. "But maybe not. I don't know. Probably not."

"You know we're very cute, right?" Emory smiled.

"I'm not sure," Brunelle replied. "I bet some people find us annoying."

"They probably find you annoying," Emory suggested, "not me."

"That does seem likely," Brunelle agreed.

"Are you two done?" Chen called out from the front porch. "We found something."

Brunelle feigned disappointment. "Oh no. I better go talk to Larry. You're going to stay here, right?"

Emory smirked. "Sure."

"Cool." Brunelle punctuated his exit with finger-guns and hurried to the porch to check in with Chen. "What's up?"

Chen held up a large clear plastic evidence bag. Inside was a folded document.

"What's that?" Brunelle asked.

"A life insurance policy," Chen explained. "Taken out last month on Charlie Rycroft. Payable to a Katherine Sommers."

"Katie," Brunelle realized. "The ex-fiancée girlfriend."

"And it's at the brother's house, not hers," Chen pointed out.

"Sounds like you need to talk with Katie Sommers," Brunelle said.

"Sounds like you may have more than one defendant to charge," Chen returned. "You want to tag along again?"

"Why not?" Brunelle answered. "Just let me check in with my better half."

He walked back toward Emory but only close enough to be able to yell to her across the front lawn.

"Rain check on that dinner thing tonight." He jerked a thumb over his shoulder toward Chen. "I have to babysit Larry on the next stage of this investigation. Super sorry."

Emory shook her head but couldn't suppress a grin. "See? Annoying."

Brunelle shrugged and pointed at himself. "Lawyer."

CHAPTER 7

Katie Sommers lived in Seattle, although not the fancy South Lake Union neighborhood of her ex-fiancé's brother. Her apartment was in the mundane Roosevelt neighborhood, tucked forgettably between the bustling University District and the recreational Green Lake area. Brunelle was pretty sure he'd been to a Thai restaurant there one time, but it looked like it had closed down. So had the coffee shop across the street. The drugstore was still there though, as were the three floors of apartments atop it. Chen and Brunelle stepped off the elevator and made their way to apartment 205, home of the dead man's girlfriend.

Maybe, Brunelle thought.

It was definitely her apartment. He just wasn't convinced she was really his girlfriend anymore. And not just because he was dead.

Chen squared up to the door and knocked while Brunelle slid off to the side. It was Chen's conversation to have, not his. And to whatever extent Katie Sommers might be hesitant to open her door to a strange man she could barely make out through the fisheye lens of the peephole, that hesitancy would only be increased by seeing two strange men standing outside her door.

But maybe one was enough after all to keep her from opening her door. There was no response to Chen's knock. He waited that amount of time you wait until it's appropriate to knock again and did so. Still no response. And no sound from inside the apartment either. Chen waited that slightly less amount of time between the second and third knocks and knocked again. Still nothing.

Chen frowned, then reached for the door handle.

"You got a warrant for that, officer?" Brunelle chided him. They both knew he didn't.

"Exigent circumstances," Chen claimed. "Maybe I want to make sure she's okay."

"She's not there," came a voice from down the hall.

Brunelle and Chen both turned to see a middle-aged woman standing in the doorway of the next apartment, a laundry basket propped on her hip.

"She left this morning, crying," the woman continued. "I ran into her when she was leaving. She could barely lock the deadbolt behind her. She said her boyfriend was dead and her ex-boyfriend was in jail."

"Wow, crazy," Brunelle responded.

The woman took a moment to size them up. "You guys cops or something?"

"Or something," Brunelle answered. "Did she say when she'd be back?"

The woman shook her head. "No. I'm not even sure she's coming back. She had a bag with her."

"Damn it." Chen frowned. "We should have moved

quicker."

Brunelle wasn't so sure. "Maybe she'll lead us to something she wouldn't have otherwise if you'd come here sooner. It's not like you can't track her down. She probably checked into a hotel using a credit card."

"Or we just get a warrant for her phone's GPS location," Chen suggested.

"Yeah, or that." Brunelle sighed. The detectives were growing up so fast.

CHAPTER 8

It turned out Katie was even more tech savvy than a mid-50s homicide detective. She had turned her phone off, along with any other electronic devices that might be tracked. Even Brunelle's old-school credit card inquiry only managed to confirm she took $500 cash from an ATM after the tearful goodbye with her neighbor. She had dropped completely off the grid. Two days later, as Brunelle prepared for the afternoon hearing where he would have to explain to the judge whether he was charging or releasing Matthew Rycroft, no one had seen hide nor hair of Katie Sommers.

Until Brunelle got a phone call from an old nemesis. That meant a colleague. A lawyer. Ergo, annoying. A defense lawyer; ergo, doubly annoying. But one Brunelle had mostly avoided tangling with over the years, although through no fault of his own.

"Brunelle," he answered his phone. He still wanted to add 'homicides' after that every time he answered the phone, but Chen had shamed him out of it.

"Dave!" enthused the voice on the other side. "Long

time, no convictions, huh?"

Brunelle lowered his head into his hand. It was Nicholas Nicholson, local attorney and all-around irritating human being. They had graduated law school at the same time and while Brunelle built up a career as a prosecutor, Nicholson was building up his law firm. He was a hell of a businessman, it turned out, but his business model was high fees, low quality work, and staffing the firm with brand new lawyers he could underpay and fire after a year or two. No one actually got Nicholas Nicholson to represent them in court; they got one of his flunky associates. But it was Nicholson's name over the door.

"What do you want, Nick?" Brunelle grumbled. "I've got work to do. Shouldn't you be calling the DUI unit? Or drugs maybe? I do homicides and you don't do homicides."

"You're right, Dave. As usual." Nicholson offered an overly sincere laugh. "I don't do homicides. But sometimes I do things adjacent to homicides."

"What are you talking about?" Brunelle really had no patience for bottom-feeders like Nicholson. He rarely had to deal with the hustlers since he got to homicides. You don't win a homicide case with a winning smile and a practiced pitch to an overworked misdemeanor prosecutor.

"I heard you might be looking for a certain girlfriend of a certain murder victim," Nicholson explained. "Katie Sommers. Does that name ring any bells?"

Of course it did. Warning bells. There was no way it was good news that Nicholas Nicholson was calling him about Katie Sommers.

"Maybe," Brunelle allowed. "What do you know about her?"

"I know she's my client," Nicholson answered, "and I know she would like to cooperate with the prosecution."

Brunelle waited for it.

"In exchange for immunity, of course," Nicholson added.

There it was.

"Immunity?' Brunelle repeated back. "For murder? You know I can't do that."

"Well, actually, we both know you can," Nicholson said. "You have absolute authority to make that decision. But no, I'm not asking for immunity from murder. My client didn't murder anyone, and she wasn't an accomplice to anyone else murdering someone. But there is a possibility, remote as it may be, that some overzealous prosecutor might misinterpret her actions as somehow rendering criminal assistance to a murderer—unknowingly, I assure you—and we both know rendering assistance to a murderer is not only a crime, but a serious felony."

"Not as serious as murder," Brunelle pointed out.

"Correct, Mr. Brunelle, correct," Nicholson replied. "You always were the smart one, even back in law school."

"We never had a class together in law school, Nick," Brunelle sighed, "and if we had, you wouldn't have said that just now."

"It was a guess, Dave," Nicholson admitted. "You always seemed like a smart guy. Be smart on this case. Give my gal immunity and let her tell you what she knows."

Brunelle shook his head, even if just to himself. "No, that's not how it works. If she wants to tell me what she knows, great. I'm more than happy to listen. But I'm not giving her immunity before she makes a statement. What if I give her immunity and she confesses to being the one and only murderer? What then? How do I explain that to my boss, let alone the victim's family?"

"Isn't the victim's family your current suspect?" Nicholson reminded him.

That was a good point. But it wasn't the main point. "I've done this before, and I'm sure I'll do this again," Brunelle said. "I will give your client transactional immunity for her statement only. I will agree that anything she says in that statement can't be used against her in my case-in-chief at trial. But I'm not giving her blanket immunity. If she says something that leads to other evidence of wrongdoing or if I find other evidence that links her to the murder, I'm charging her and I'm convicting her. Understood?"

There was a long pause on the other end of the line. Finally, Nicholson asked, "Did you really just say 'other evidence of wrongdoing'? This isn't a 1970s cop show, Dave."

"Don't push me, Nick," Brunelle warned. He glanced at the clock. "If we're going to do this, we need to do it now. I've got a second appearance on my prime suspect in four hours. If your client has evidence to support a murder charge, I need it before then. I know you know where she is, even if my cops don't. Can she and you be at my office in one hour? I'll have the lead detective here and we'll take a recorded statement. If it helps me, she'll get the benefit of that. If it doesn't—"

"She'll likely be arrested by your detective," Nicholson finished. "I know. Although that would turn her into a defendant with the right to remain silent, instead of a witness who has to testify if you subpoena her."

"Which is why she better say something I find valuable," Brunelle replied.

"I understand the stakes, Dave," Nicholson assured. "I wouldn't have called you if I didn't think this would go in my client's favor."

"One hour, Nick," Brunelle instructed. "Don't be late."

CHAPTER 9

"He knows I'm going to arrest her, right?" Chen asked Brunelle 55 minutes later, as they stood waiting in the conference room off the main lobby of the prosecutor's offices. "As soon as she's done talking."

Brunelle nodded. "I think we're all kind of expecting that. Even her. But Nicholson must think she's got something great to tell us if he thinks she can talk us out of putting her in a cell right next to her ex-fiancé."

"Exactly." Chen nodded. Then, after a moment. "I mean, they segregate the inmates by sex, obviously. She wouldn't be right next to him. There's like a whole separate wing for the females."

Brunelle rolled his eyes. "I was speaking figuratively."

"I know." Chen shrugged. "Just trying to be accurate. I'm a detective, you know. Just the facts, ma'am, and all that."

Brunelle thought for a moment. "I wish it was going to be just facts. But I'm pretty sure it's going to be a paltry helping of facts, wrapped in lies, and hidden beneath a layer of misdirection and malintent."

"That's very poetic," Chen admired. "Very lawyerly."

Brunelle narrowed his eyes at his friend. "Is that a compliment?"

"The 'poetic' part was," Chen answered.

Before Brunelle could press, the front desk receptionist appeared in the doorway to the conference room. "Your appointment is here, Mr. Brunelle. Should I bring them back?"

"Yes, please," Brunelle answered. He looked to Chen. "Here we go. You ready?"

Chen put his fists on his hips. "I was born ready."

Brunelle laughed but he didn't get the chance to make a witty remark.

"Dave!" Nicholson practically shouted as he walked into the conference room with his client. He was dressed to the nines in a bespoke tailored suit and leather loafers. His personality had a way of sucking all of the oxygen out of a room, and not in a good way. In contrast, Sommers was quiet and unassuming, but she still held an air of confidence about her. She seemed appropriately concerned given the general enormity of the situation, but she didn't seem scared. Brunelle didn't know if that meant she was confident in her innocence, or just another psychopathic Seattle techie. Either way, she was tall, blonde and pretty. Brunelle could see why the Rycroft brothers would fight over her.

"Great to see you again." Nicholson clapped his hands together. "We ready to do this?"

Brunelle nodded toward the single piece of paper he had placed on the conference table. "You tell me. That's the agreement. It limits her immunity to this interview and this investigation only. If she confesses to any unrelated crimes, I can prosecute those. If she gets charged based on independent evidence and she testifies in that trial differently from what she says here, I can use this statement to show she's lying."

"Is that all?" Nicholson chuckled, a bit more nervously than Brunelle would have expected.

"And no promises," Brunelle added. "She tells us everything, no strings attached. If I believe her and if I think it's helpful, then I might offer not to charge her in exchange for her testimony against the principal actors. Or maybe I believe her and I think it's helpful, but I don't need it. In that case, thanks for coming, but no prize behind door number two."

Sommers glanced around the conference room. "Where is door number two?"

"Sorry, Katie," Nicholson apologized for Brunelle. "It's an old reference to an even older T.V. show."

"It's not that old of a reference," Brunelle muttered to himself. But Chen gave him a '*Yes, it is*' look.

"Fine," Brunelle huffed. "Let's just get started. Review the document with your client. Once she signs it, Detective Chen will turn on the tape recorder and we'll get started."

"Um, there's no tape, Dave," Chen reminded him. "It's just a recorder."

Brunelle sighed heavily. "Whatever. Let's just get to it, please. I have other things to do today."

Not least of which was to decide whether the information Katie Sommers gave them was going to be enough to push the murder charge against her ex-boyfriend across the finish line.

Nicholson sat down at the table with his client, and they reviewed the form. It wasn't exactly a standard form, but Brunelle had done it enough times that it was saved on his computer. Once Nicholson explained the form to his client and she signed it at his direction, Brunelle and Chen joined them at the conference table and Chen started the not-tape recorder.

He began with a recitation of the people present, the date and time, and the case number. It was a voluntary interview, so he didn't have to read Sommers her *Miranda* rights, but he did it anyway, just in case, followed by reading Brunelle's snitch agreement into the recorder as well. That all took a while. Too long. Brunelle's patience was severely tested by the time they finally got to whatever Katie Sommers had actually come to say. At least she got right to it.

"I hate to say it," she said it anyway, "but I think Matt probably did it. He never really got over me."

Modest, Brunelle frowned to himself. In addition to assessing whether Sommers was telling the truth, Brunelle was also assessing what kind of witness she would be if he had to build his case on her testimony. He wanted her to be likeable.

"I'm pretty hard to get over," she added, apparently unironically.

Nope, Brunelle thought.

"I'm sure he was jealous enough to kill his brother."

"Thank you for sharing your opinion with us, Ms. Sommers," Brunelle said as he glared sideways at Nicholson, "but witnesses aren't usually allowed to just take the stand and spout off unsupported opinions. It's kind of Evidence Rules 101. Do you have any actual facts you could share with us? Maybe like where Matt was on the night of the murder. Or where you were, for that matter."

"Whoa, wait a second." Sommers raised her palms at that. "Testimony? Where was I when he was murdered? Like, do I have an alibi?" She looked over to Nicholson. "You never said anything about having to testify or needing an alibi."

"Whoa, calm down, Katie," Nicholson tried.

Brunelle was old, but he knew not to tell a woman to 'calm down' anymore.

"Calm down?" Sommers spat back at him. "Did you really just tell a woman to 'calm down'? Oh, I knew this was a mistake. Fine." She turned back to Brunelle. "You want to know where I was when Charlie was murdered? I was with Matt, alright?"

"Matt?" Brunelle said. "Matt Rycroft? But you just said you thought he did it."

"I do," Sommers narrowed her eyes at him, "because he left in the middle of the night for no reason. I thought he was cheating on me, but now I know what really happened. He thinks I didn't notice, but I did and—"

"Hold on," Brunelle interrupted. "You were spending the night with your boyfriend's brother? Your ex-fiancé?"

Sommers jabbed a finger at him. "Don't you dare judge me. It's complicated."

"Um, hey, Dave," Nicholson interrupted, "can you give me a minute to talk with my client? Privately?"

"I don't have a minute, Nick," Brunelle responded. "You were supposed to talk with her before you got here."

"I'm going to need to talk with her some more, I think," Nicholson said. "This went in a little bit of a different direction than what I was expecting."

"You weren't expecting me to ask her where she was?" Brunelle questioned. "Or follow up when she said she was with the fucking defendant?"

"Good points, Dave. Good points." Nicholson smiled broadly, like a con man looking for the exit. "Why don't we call this a good first attempt and let's circle back in a few days to see where we're at?"

"So, we're done?" Brunelle asked. He glanced at Chen, who frowned back at him.

Nicholson nodded and stood up. "I would say so. I'll speak with my client to see if there's anything more we can do to assist you."

Brunelle stood up too. He didn't say anything to Nicholson, but offered a single sharp nod. Then he turned to Chen and shook his head almost imperceptibly. There wasn't enough to arrest her. He didn't need two suspects in custody pending additional evidence.

Chen remained seated, standing down from the post-interview arrest plan, and allowed Brunelle to escort Nicholson and his client out of the prosecutor's office.

When Brunelle returned, they planned their next moves.

"I'll follow her," Chen said. "See where she goes, and who she meets."

"And I'll draft the complaint to file murder charges against Matthew Rycroft," Brunelle said. "She didn't give us much, but she blew away the alibi he's going to offer."

"He left in the middle of the night," Chen repeated Sommers's words.

Brunelle nodded and allowed himself a slight smile. "He left in the middle of the night."

CHAPTER 10

There wasn't time for Chen to draft up an official report of their aborted interview with Katie Sommers, but that didn't mean Brunelle couldn't tell Matt Rycroft's attorney orally. In fact, he probably was required to. The flow of information in criminal cases was pretty simple: prosecutors had to tell the defense attorney everything and the defense attorney didn't have to tell the prosecutor anything, at least not until the very last moment. But prosecutors had to disclose things as soon as possible and he'd been to more than one training where they learned about some poor prosecutor from the other side of the country who had lost his bar license because he forgot to tell the defense attorney something a witness said in some random phone call that didn't get documented. So, when he walked into the criminal presiding courtroom just before 1:00 p.m. that afternoon, Brunelle made a beeline to Jessica Edwards, the top homicide attorney in the public defender's office.

"Hey, Jess," he greeted her. They'd been friends and enemies for over a dozen years. They weren't just on a first name basis; it was nicknames. "You here on the Rycroft arraignment?"

"Hey, Dave," she returned the nickname. "I was, but I guess he hired private counsel."

"Really?" Brunelle was a bit surprised. Gone were the days when only the truly indigent got public defenders. Retainers on a murder case were so high, anyone with just a regular retail job—like floor salesman at P.N.W. Outfitters— wasn't going to be able to afford a lawyer.

"I guess so." Edwards pointed to a tall blonde woman near the entrance to the courtroom. "That's her. Amanda West."

"Never heard of her." Brunelle frowned.

"Me either," Edwards agreed. "But she came up to me a minute ago to introduce herself and let me know she was filing a notice of appearance on the case."

"Not to be indelicate," Brunelle started, "but she looks a little old to be just starting out."

It was indelicate, but it was also accurate. Amanda West appeared to be almost as old as he was. New lawyers were twenty-somethings, not forty-somethings. She wore a suit fancier than everyone else, had more jewelry on than everyone else, and her hair was done up more than anyone else. If she hadn't stuck out for Brunelle not knowing her—he knew everyone by then, it seemed—she would have stood out for looking like she belonged in a courtroom in Los Angeles rather than the Rainy City.

"Don't be sexist, Dave," Edwards warned.

"I'm not being sexist," Brunelle defended. "Her appearance has nothing to do with her gender."

Edwards grinned. "Let's all look forward to the day when that's true. Until then, try not to comment on a woman's age or appearance."

Brunelle frowned again. "Can I think it?"

"Could I stop you?" Edwards laughed.

"Unlikely," Brunelle admitted. "I guess, I better go introduce myself."

Amanda West was also attractive. That done-up hair was a honey blonde and that fancy suit was tailored over a pleasant figure. Not that Brunelle would comment out loud on that.

"Hello, Ms. West?" He stepped up to her and extended a hand. "I'm Dave Brunelle, the prosecutor on the Rycroft case. Ms. Edwards said you'll be representing Mr. Rycroft?"

West shook Brunelle's hand. She had a nice grip. "Nice to meet you, Mr. Brunelle. Yes, I have been retained by Mr. Rycroft."

"I don't think we've met before," Brunelle said. "Are you new to Seattle, or have I just missed seeing you around the courthouse?"

"A little of both perhaps," West answered. "I'm not new to Seattle. I'm Seattle born and raised. But I am newer to the legal profession. This is sort of a second career for me. I'm sure you'll be seeing more of me now that I've got my foot in the door."

That explained it. She must have low-balled the fee to get hired so she could get some experience. Rycroft probably called a half-dozen lawyers and picked the one who charged the least. Well, you get what you pay for.

"Well, then, welcome aboard," Brunelle replied. "I'll look forward to getting to know you over the course of the case."

West forced a tight smile. "This is the second appearance, I understand. Will you be filing charges today or releasing my client?"

"I'm afraid we're filing charges." Brunelle pulled copies of the charging documents out of his file and offered them to her. "One count of murder in the first degree."

West frowned, but accepted the paperwork. "Would you change your mind if I told you my client has an alibi for that night?"

"Ah, right on time." Brunelle chuckled.

West frowned. "What is that supposed to mean?"

"You'll understand when you read the police reports," Brunelle assured. "I knew he would have an alibi today."

West's frown was joined by knitted eyebrows. "How could you know about his alibi? We only discussed it privately just this morning. He told me he didn't make a statement to the police."

"He told the police, and me," Brunelle explained, "that he would come up with an alibi. By today. And now I guess he has."

"Well, I can assure you, Mr. Brunelle," West regained her expression and tilted her chin up slightly, "Mr. Rycroft's coworker will vouch for his whereabouts on the night in question."

Brunelle's own eyebrows descended a bit. "Coworker?" That was a weird way to describe your ex-fiancée/brother's girlfriend/cheating mistress.

"James Crossero. They work together at P.N.W. Outfitters," West explained. "She extracted a document from her own file and handed it to Brunelle. "As you can see from his sworn statement, Mr. Crossero will say that Mr. Rycroft was with him the entire evening, playing online videogames late into the next morning."

Brunelle grimaced. He probably should have led with

the whole 'Katie Sommers blew up your client's alibi' thing. "Yeah, about that. We just did an interview of your client's ex-fiancée, Katie Sommers, who also happens to be the victim's current girlfriend. She said your client was with her that night, until he wasn't."

West's face dropped. She opened her mouth to say something but was cut off by the call of the bailiff.

"All rise! The King County Superior Court is now in session, The Honorable Susan Park presiding!"

Brunelle smiled at his opponent and nodded toward the front of the courtroom. "If you're ready, we can handle your matter first."

West took a moment then shook the fluster out of her head. "Of course I'm ready."

Brunelle offered a simple, "Great," then headed toward the bench, West in tow.

"The parties are ready, Your Honor," he informed the judge, "for the arraignment on the matter of *The State of Washington versus Matthew Rycroft*."

Brunelle nodded toward the jail guard at the secure door to the holding cells just off the courtroom, letting him know to escort Rycroft into the courtroom.

Judge Park glanced over the courtroom. "And who is representing Mr. Rycroft?"

"I am, Your Honor." West stepped up to the bar. "Amanda West on behalf of Matthew Rycroft."

"Ah." The judge nodded down to her. "Nice to meet you, Ms.—did you say West?"

"Yes, Your Honor," she confirmed. "Amanda West."

"Nice to meet you, Ms. West," Judge Park said. Then after a glance to the opened cell door, "Here comes your client now."

Rycroft was dressed in red jail scrubs. The inmates were color coded by outfit. Green were the 'trustees'—usually being held on misdemeanors and well-behaved enough to be allowed to walk outside to throw out the trash or wheel laundry to and from the trucks. Gray meant you were just an average inmate, not causing trouble but not getting any benefits either. White meant super-scary, top security, will try to bite your face off if you unhandcuff them. Those usually came to court wearing a spit-guard over their face and sometimes even strapped into a wheelchair so they could barely move while the guard rolled them into court. Red usually meant either some disciplinary problems, or the most serious charges. It was a warning to the guard, not to worry about being attacked necessarily, but to make sure they didn't take their eyes off someone who might try to make a run for it at the first opportunity.

Rycroft didn't seem like the kind of guy to make trouble, and he didn't bear any obvious bruises to his face from being 'escorted to the ground' by jail staff. It was just that he was looking at a Murder One charge. Something Brunelle was about to make official.

"Your Honor, I'm handing forward the complaint in the matter," he announced as he handed the document to the bailiff, "charging the defendant with one count of murder in the first degree. The State would ask the Court to arraign the defendant on the charge and then to be heard regarding conditions of release."

"Thank you, Mr. Brunelle," Judge Park said as she accepted the paperwork from the bailiff. "Ms. West, have you received copies of the complaint?"

West raised the papers in her hand slightly. "Yes, Your

Honor."

A more experienced criminal defense attorney would have followed that up with the standard recitation of, 'We acknowledge receipt, waive a formal reading, and enter a plea of not guilty'. But West just stood there, looking almost as clueless as her client standing, wide-eyed next to her.

"Would you like the Court to read the complaint out loud in open court, or would you waive a formal reading, counsel?" The words of the question were neutral, but the intonation made clear the judge's preference.

"Uh, yes, Your Honor," West stammered, "we would waive a formal reading of the complaint."

Judge Park waited another beat, then had to ask, "And do you ask the Court to enter a plea of not guilty on behalf of your client?"

"Um, yes, Your Honor." West nodded. "My client pleads not guilty."

Judge Park nodded to herself. "A plea of not guilty will be entered. I will hear from the State regarding conditions of release."

It was really more like conditions of not-release. At least if Brunelle got his way, which seemed likely given the seriousness of the charges and the inexperience of his opponent.

"Thank you, Your Honor," he began, and got right to the point, "the State is asking the Court to set bail in the amount of one million dollars. The defendant is charged with the crime of murder in the first degree, a most serious offense, and one that carries with it a significant prison sentence, if convicted. Although the defendant may have some ties to the local community, one of the most significant of these would have been his brother, but that's the person he's alleged to have murdered. Therefore, we don't think family connections carry as much weight as they might in other cases. The State believes he is a flight risk and also a risk to the greater community, given the nature of the charges. As the Court is aware, bail in a first-degree murder case is regularly set at one million dollars and there is nothing about this case which would suggest deviating downward from that standard. Accordingly, we believe bail in the amount of one million dollars is appropriate and ask the Court to set it at that amount. Thank you."

Judge Park nodded along, then turned to West. "I will hear now from the defense."

"Thank you, Your Honor," West replied. "The defense would ask the Court to consider releasing Mr. Rycroft on his personal recognizance."

That was definitely a rookie mistake, Brunelle thought. No judge was going to P.R. a murder defendant. Ever. Better to ask for a low bail that your client could actually post. Then again, maybe Rycroft used up all his funds hiring West. He should have just gone with the public defender. Based on what Brunelle had seen so far, Edwards was ten times the lawyer West was.

"Mr. Rycroft is not a flight risk," West continued. "He does indeed have family in the Seattle area. Not just his late brother, but also parents and other family. And I should remind the Court that Mr. Rycroft is presumed innocent, so concluding he doesn't have strong ties to the community because of what he is accused of doing would be highly inappropriate."

Brunelle winced slightly. Judges didn't usually like being 'reminded' of things. They know a defendant is presumed innocent. So, it comes across as suggesting they don't care and won't follow the law. Which is pretty much the worst allegation you can make against a judge.

"I understand the law, counsel," Judge Park warned West. Again, the warning wasn't in the words, but the tone was unmistakable.

"I know you do, Your Honor," West tried to dodge, "and that's why I'm hoping the Court will agree to release Mr. Rycroft on his promise to appear. He is presumed innocent. He has an alibi. He has ties to the community. He has gone to the trouble and expense of retaining a private attorney. I can assure the Court that he will come back to appear in court so that he can prove his innocence."

Another mistake. Lawyers shouldn't vouch for their clients. West was new enough at criminal that she hadn't had a client burn her yet, but if she stuck with it long enough, she would.

Brunelle didn't care about most of West's argument—it was boilerplate defense attorney babble—but he didn't want to let the alibi claim pass by unchallenged. That was the sort of thing that might sway a judge. Presumed innocent or not, judges set million-dollar bails because they figured the defendant was probably guilty or the State wouldn't, or shouldn't, be prosecuting them. An alibi could cast doubt on that, which could give a judge pause when ordering, essentially, that the defendant be jailed in advance of his conviction.

"If I might respond briefly, Your Honor," Brunelle interjected. "I just wanted the Court to know that the State disputes the defendant's alibi." He disdainfully shook the copy of the sworn statement West had given him. "We have a witness who will directly refute the defendant's claims regarding his whereabouts that night."

"May I respond?" West asked.

But Judge Park shook her head. "I don't think that will

be necessary, Ms. West. This is neither the time nor the place to litigate the merits of the charges or the defenses in this case. I will not be considering Mr. Brunelle's statements regarding your client's alibi, but neither will I be considering your assertions in that regard."

Mission accomplished, thought Brunelle.

"The Court will set bail at one million dollars, as requested by the State," Judge Park announced. "Next case."

Brunelle, having won, was only too happy to step away from the bar, victory in hand. West hesitated, but then had no choice but to vacate her spot as the jail guard grabbed her client and the next defense attorney slid into place in front of her. Brunelle was ready to head back to his office, but West grabbed him by the arm.

"I really think you should have told me about that witness of yours before I told you what my client's alibi was," she complained.

Brunelle shrugged. "You didn't give me a chance. It was the first thing out of your mouth. And anyway, you probably should have read all the police reports before deciding what your defense was going to be," he advised. "That way, you could tailor your lies to fit the evidence. But like you said, you're new at this."

CHAPTER 11

Matt Rycroft being successfully locked away for the foreseeable future, Brunelle's attention turned back to Katie Sommers, and what Chen might have found out from tailing her that afternoon.

"Nothing," Chen admitted when Brunelle called him. "Not a damn thing."

"Really?" Brunelle was disappointed. He wasn't sure if he should be surprised.

"Really," Chen confirmed. "I followed her to her work. She stayed there all day. Then I followed her home. She didn't even stop for gas. This has been the least interesting stakeout I've ever been on."

"Maybe she'll go out later tonight," Brunelle suggested.

"Maybe I'll miss it," Chen returned, "because I'm going home now to have dinner with my wife."

Brunelle frowned but nodded, none of which Chen could see over the phone, of course. He could hardly blame Chen, and he wasn't even sure what he expected to find out anyway.

"Well, at least we tried," Brunelle said. "Maybe—"

"Wait." Chen interrupted. "She's coming out of the building again. She's headed for her car."

"She parked on the street?" Brunelle asked. "There's no garage?"

"I'll speak with the property company about their parking arrangements later, Dave," Chen sighed. "Right now, I think I'll focus on where Ms. Sommers is headed."

"You're going to miss dinner," Brunelle warned.

"Eh, it was leftovers anyway," Chen replied.

"No, it wasn't," Brunelle knew, "but thanks."

"Don't mention it," Chen said. "And it'll be leftovers by the time I get home."

Brunelle could hardly argue with that. "Where is she headed?"

"Freeway," Chen answered. "I-5. Southbound."

"Toward downtown," Brunelle said.

"Maybe," Chen responded. "Let's see what exit she takes."

The exit she took was just north of downtown. Mercer Street. The South Lake Union District. The victim's neighborhood.

"Is she really going to the dead guy's apartment?" Brunelle could hardly believe it. "Returning to the scene of the crime?"

"Not sure about returning to it," Chen said. "Don't we think she was at Matt's house in Bellevue? But she is definitely parking across the street and getting out of her car. I need to swing around and park without her noticing me."

"Let me know how that goes," Brunelle said.

"Not great," Chen reported. "I think she saw me. I don't know, maybe not."

"What's she doing?"

"Looks like she's entering a security code at the front entrance," Chen answered. "Yep, she just pulled the front door open and headed inside."

"Guess they haven't changed the code since her fiancé was murdered," Brunelle said.

"Boyfriend," Chen corrected. "Matt was the fiancé. Charlie hadn't reached that level yet."

"Didn't reach it ever," Brunelle observed. "You going in after her?"

"To prevent her from contaminating the crime scene?" Chen asked rhetorically. "Yes. Even if I weren't following her, I'm not letting her go into that apartment."

"Or maybe do let her go in," Brunelle suggested, "and catch her red-handed doing whatever she went there to do."

Chen agreed that might be a wise course of action, then hung up on Brunelle in order to execute it. Brunelle would have to wait for Chen to call back before he learned what Katie Sommers was doing at the site of her boyfriend's murder. But he didn't have to wait as long as he'd expected to.

"You're done already?" he asked when Chen called him back less than ten minutes later. "What happened? What was she doing in Charlie's apartment?"

"Good question," Chen replied. "I have no idea. She wasn't in there."

"She wasn't in there?" Brunelle repeated, incredulous. "Where was she?"

"I don't know," Chen admitted. "I went straight up to Rycroft's apartment. It was locked but I still had the key from the landlord. I opened it up and went inside. You know, they still haven't replaced the carpet? That smell is hard enough to get out. They don't want it getting into the curtains or the wood."

Brunelle supposed that was true enough. "And she wasn't in there?"

"Nope," Chen confirmed. "Like I said, the door was locked, but I figured she probably had a key to her boyfriend's apartment, so I searched it, looking for her. I checked every square inch. She wasn't in there."

"Did she hear you coming?"

"I don't think so," Chen said. "There's only one way in or out. Unless you count the balcony, but I checked there first."

"You checked the balcony first?" Brunelle questioned.

"I've been doing this a long time, Dave," Chen sighed. "I know where people hide when the cops walk in on them. She wasn't there."

Brunelle thought for a moment. "Then where was she?"

"That's the sixty-four-thousand-dollar question," Chen replied.

Brunelle just shook his head. Not because he didn't get the reference. Because he did.

"We really are old, aren't we?"

CHAPTER 12

That was twice Katie Sommers had avoided them. The only time she actually talked with them, Nick Nicholson had gotten in the way, and she had terminated the conversation almost immediately. Still, the one piece of information they had managed to get from her then was probably the most important information they could have gotten: Matt Rycroft's whereabouts at the time of his brother's murder. Or at least his not-whereabouts. He wasn't with Katie Sommers.

He must have known she would rat him out, and that was why he told his bargain-basement defense attorney the new story about Jimmy Crispado or whoever. Of course, that begged the question why Jimmy the Coworker would sign a statement he knew was false. Who was that good of friends with a coworker? Were they more than friends? Was that why it hadn't worked out with Katie?

All of those questions, and more, were unlikely to be answered, Brunelle knew, by just sitting at his desk and thinking about them. There was more investigation to be done, and with the charges formally filed, Brunelle was finally in a position to help. Chen would follow up on Katie's story. Brunelle would follow up on Jimmy's. Chen would do whatever it was cops did in the field. And Brunelle would do what lawyers did in the courthouse: argue with other lawyers.

The first pretrial conference in the case of *The State of Washington versus Matthew Rycroft* was scheduled for a week after the arraignment. Brunelle and Amanda West would meet in the conference room outside the criminal presiding courtroom and see if they couldn't settle the case. They couldn't, of course. Brunelle was saying Rycroft murdered his brother in Seattle and West was saying her client was in Bellevue the whole night. Those were pretty irreconcilable differences. But the pretrial was mandatory, so they had to make it look good for the kids.

"Ms. West," Brunelle greeted her in the cacophony of what the experienced criminal bar affectionately called 'The Pit'. He doubted she knew that term yet. She was seated at a large table off to one side, but not quite against the wall. Next to her were several other prosecutors and defense attorneys, wheeling and dealing. They were handling the car thefts and drug cases, with far better chances of reaching an agreement somewhere between what the defendant deserved and what they wanted. But the gap between a few decades in prison or simply walking out the door was too wide to bridge with professional courtesy and a desire to get to the next case on your desk. "It's nice to see you again."

"You too, Mr. Brunelle," West replied as he sat down next to her in the one chair at the table that was still free. "I saved you a seat."

"So I see," Brunelle acknowledged. "Thank you. Hopefully, it'll be worth it. Are you still going with the 'I was with my coworker all night' story? Or do you have a new sworn statement for me? Perhaps one from his gardener? Or the neighbor a few doors down that he sees infrequently if they happen to go to the mailboxes at the same time? What about that guy he rode the bus with that one time?"

West managed a pained smile. "You know, Mr. Brunelle, after the arraignment, I asked around about you. Reviews were mixed, but overall they painted a generally positive picture. At least a professional one. I must say, it's not very becoming of a prosecutor to resort to trash-talking. Yours is a nobler profession than that, or so you all like to claim."

Brunelle couldn't help but feel a bit chastened. His cocky grin faded.

"Perhaps, rather than making fun of my client's claim of innocence," West suggested, "you could accept it in the spirit it's offered and actually investigate it."

A fair point, he had to admit.

"I mean," West continued, "is your witness so much more reliable? Do you really put that much faith in her?"

Brunelle nodded. "Okay. Fine. I'll concede your point. Or at least one of them. I definitely want to establish once and for all where your client was that night."

"If you do that, Mr. Brunelle," West said, "I am confident you will agree to dismiss the case against my client."

"Unlikely," Brunelle replied, "but I won't prejudge it. If I'm convinced he didn't do it, of course I won't proceed. Can you promise the same if I prove the opposite?"

"Promise I'll stop defending my client if you disprove his alibi?" West restated the proposition.

"Yes," Brunelle confirmed.

"Absolutely not," West almost laughed. But it wasn't

really a laughing matter. "Of course not. That's not what defense attorneys do."

"I know." Brunelle nodded. "And that's why we prosecutors think ours is the nobler profession."

CHAPTER 13

Brunelle didn't really think being a prosecutor was the nobler profession. Well, maybe he did, but he also respected the job defense attorneys had to do. He wouldn't want to do it, but if they didn't do it, it wouldn't be long before his profession, unchecked, became anything but noble.

Their job was to defend their clients, at all costs, regardless of the truth. His job was to seek out that truth, regardless of the consequences to his case. A dismissal for the right reasons was as much a victory as a conviction. At least, in theory.

But he was still hoping Chen could disprove Rycroft's claim he spent the night with his buddy Crossero.

He also wanted to bolster Katie's story that Matt was with her until he wasn't. The challenge with that was that Katie Sommers was represented by a lawyer, and the Rules of Professional Conduct prohibited lawyers from directly contacting people they knew were represented by other lawyers. That meant further inquiry into Katie Sommers's claims had to go through Nick Nicholson. And that meant Brunelle was going to have to do it, while Chen would take the Crossero angle. They would debrief again after one or the other of them had either proved or disproved the dueling alibis proffered by their targets.

Chen agreed to follow up with Crossero. Brunelle picked up the phone and dialed Nicholson's number.

"Good afternoon. Law Offices of Nicholas Nicholson," answered the receptionist. "Are you a prospective new client?"

Brunelle had to hand it to Nicholson. He wasn't shy about using his law degree as a business tool. A widget maker, as it were. He wasn't in it for the greater concepts of good and evil, justice and injustice, liberty versus security and man's inhumanity to man. He was in it for the money. For him, a law degree was just a glorified trade certificate. And Brunelle knew he wasn't completely wrong.

"Um, no," Brunelle answered. "My name is David Brunelle. I'm a prosecutor with the King County Prosecutor's Office. I'd like to speak with Mr. Nicholson, please. We have a case in common."

"I'm afraid Mr. Nicholson isn't available right now," the woman on the other end of the line said, with obvious practice. "Would you like his voicemail?"

Brunelle considered that option but only long enough to reject it. "No, thank you. I'll just try again later."

"All right then," the receptionist said in a way that communicated she would tell Brunelle the exact same thing every time he called, even if Nicholson himself were sitting on her lap while she said it. "Have a nice day."

Brunelle hung up and counted to 30. Then he dialed Nicholson's number again.

"Good afternoon. Law office of Nicholas Nicholson. Are

you a potential new client?"

"Yes," Brunelle answered. "Yes, I am."

If she could lie, he could too.

"I just got a DUI. Well, two actually," he continued. "I saw your billboard down on First Ave., and I had a buddy at work that you guys helped out and he said you were the best, and I have a credit card, well two actually, and—"

"Please hold for a moment," the receptionist interrupted, "and I will put you through to Mr. Nicholson."

"I thought so," Brunelle muttered. "Thank you."

He wondered whether he was being transferred to Nicholson's office phone or patched through to his cell, but either way, it only took a few seconds before Nicholson picked up. "This is Nick Nicholson, attorney at law. How can I help you?"

"You can set up another interview with Katie Sommers," Brunelle said, "and this time make sure she says more than two sentences."

"D—Dave," Nicholson stammered. "Dave Brunelle. Wow. So great to hear from you. Just so great. I, uh, I thought this was a new business call."

"Your receptionist thought so too," Brunelle explained. "That's the only way I could get through to you."

"You didn't happen to get a DUI or anything, did you?" Nicholson tried. "I mean, I'd hate to miss an opportunity."

"The only opportunity you're going to miss is keeping Katie Sommers out of jail," Brunelle warned. "Her ex-fiancé-slash-boyfriend got charged with murder and his lawyer gave me a completely different alibi than what your gal claimed."

"I think it's more of a booty call-slash-friends with benefits situation," Nicholson replied. "I'm not sure. Maybe it's that new polyamory thing I've been hearing about. I'm kind of curious about that actually. Have you ever—?"

"Nick," Brunelle interrupted.

"Yes?"

"Focus. Your client told the police that a murder suspect was with her the night of the murder then left, presumably to commit that murder. I relied on that statement when making the decision to charge him. If that was a lie, she committed a crime, and I am going to have her arrested for that and for anything else I can think of between now and then."

"Is that a threat?"

"Yes, absolutely," Brunelle confirmed. "Of course, it's a threat. She needs to talk with us again, and she needs to prove what she said is true."

"It's true, Dave," Nick assured him. "I promise."

"Don't promise, Nick," Brunelle chided him. "You don't know if it's true or not. You weren't there. Neither was I. Lawyers don't vouch; we present. And I need you to present her to me, to flesh out the details of this story I'm supposed to present to the jury."

"Okay, okay," Nick responded. "But what if she doesn't want to?"

"Then I'll know she lied to the lead detective in an official homicide investigation, and proceed accordingly," Brunelle explained. "I hope you got your fee up front, and that you charged enough to cover defending her in court on her own charges."

"I never discuss my fee structures," Nicholson answered, reflexively.

"I don't care about your fee structures," Brunelle said. "I care about holding a murderer responsible. You called me. You inserted your client into this. It's too late to back out now."

"Fine, fine," Nicholson agreed. He was probably antsy to get Brunelle off the phone so he could talk to a real new business client. "How much time do I have? I don't know how long it will take me to reach her."

"Two days," Brunelle decided. "Forty-eight hours. You and her in my office by the end of business Thursday. Or I start making decisions without you."

"Done and done," Nicholson agreed. "Anything for you, Dave."

"I doubt that," Brunelle replied.

"Don't doubt me, Dave," Nicholson said. "I know you don't respect me as a lawyer, but respect me as a businessman. The last thing I need is for one of my clients to get arrested *after* I got involved. I know what you need, I know how to get it to you, and now I know when you need it by. I will see you before the end of business Thursday. Thanks for your call."

Nicholson hung up and Brunelle stared at his phone for several seconds. When he'd started the conversation, he thought he was in charge, but he began to wonder whether Nicholson hadn't been playing him from the beginning. Baiting the hook with a free sample, then disappearing just when it got good. All to make the customer track him down again and absolutely demand to buy his wares. *'Take my money, damn it!'*

Brunelle frowned at himself and hoped Chen was doing better with his half of the assignment.

CHAPTER 14

Chen was not doing better with his half of the assignment. In fact, Chen wasn't doing his half of the assignment at all. He had delegated it. To Emory.

"Casey's doing your work for you?" Brunelle was more than a little surprised. "Is this case just not that important to you?"

"It's as important as every other case, Dave," Chen answered evenly.

They were in Chen's office. Brunelle had tracked him down to get a status report. He was feeling uneasy about how things were going with Nicholson, largely because he didn't really know if he knew how things were going with Nicholson. But he wasn't going to tell Chen that. He was just going to let it poison his conversation with his colleague, partner, and friend.

"My career is important to me, too," Chen continued. "My reputation is important to me. You wanted me to follow up on Rycroft's alibi. Rycroft's alibi puts him in Bellevue, with a coworker who also works in Bellevue. Bellevue P.D. already assisted us with the warrant. I'm not about to go into another jurisdiction and start making waves, especially when we've already established that they want to take the lead on anything in their city. This is one case, Dave. I'm not going to let it adversely impact my relationships with other agencies, or my superiors when those other agencies call to complain about me not respecting their jurisdiction."

Brunelle sighed heavily and ran a hand over his head. But he understood. Especially the bit about not wanting a Bellevue cop to feel disrespected, even if it was for different reasons.

"Fine," he said. "I'll call Casey. I owe her a call anyway."

"Yeah." Chen laughed. "That seems likely."

* * *

"You want me to disclose the details of an active investigation?" Emory asked incredulously when Brunelle called her.

"No," Brunelle responded instinctively to the tone of her voice. Then he thought for a moment. "Well, I mean, yes. Yes, actually. It's my investigation."

"It's your court case," Emory corrected. "It's my investigation. Cops do the investigation."

Brunelle took another second. "You're fucking with me, aren't you?"

"You wish, lawyer boy," Emory laughed.

"Maybe later?" Brunelle tried.

"Let's see how the rest of this conversation goes," Emory replied. "No promises."

"That's not a 'no'," Brunelle pointed out.

"That's not a 'no'," Emory confirmed.

Brunelle savored his possible negotiating victory, until he realized Emory had moved him off target, and rather easily at that. "Wait. What about the investigation?"

"My investigation?" Emory reminded him.

"My case," Brunelle returned. "Did Chen really ask you to check out Rycroft's alibi?"

"Yes, he did."

"How are you going to do it?" Brunelle asked.

Brunelle could hear Emory smile over the phone. "Correctly," she answered.

* * *

"Since you shoved your work off on someone else—" Brunelle started when he called Chen back.

"Since I deferred to the appropriate jurisdiction," Chen corrected.

"Tomato, potato," Brunelle replied. "Now, since you don't have anything else to do—"

"I wouldn't say that," Chen interrupted again.

"Since you aren't working on Rycroft's alibi," Brunelle adjusted his wording, "how about you help me out with the anti-alibi provided by our victim's ex-girlfriend?"

"Just girlfriend," Chen corrected again. "Matt was an ex, but Charlie was still her boyfriend."

"Maybe," Brunelle answered. "Sounds like he may have been an ex without knowing he was an ex yet."

"I suppose I can agree with that," Chen said.

"Good. So, help me test Katie Sommers's story," Brunelle continued. "She's coming in Thursday morning. I'd like you to be there."

"Fine," Chen agreed, "but just talking to her isn't going to get you what you need."

"Oh yeah," Brunelle defended, "how would you do it?"

Another grin over the phone. "Correctly."

CHAPTER 15

Katie Sommers showed up at Brunelle's office a few minutes before 11:00. Nicholson was running late, but promised he'd be there by 11:05. 11:15 at the latest. Maybe 11:20.

So, Sommers waited in the lobby and Brunelle sat in the same conference room as before, sorely tempted to talk to her without Nicholson's interference. Because that was mainly what Nicholson brought to the table: interference. Brunelle could understand why someone wrapped up in a murder, one way or another, would want to consult with a lawyer before talking to the cops, but actually hiring him meant Nicholson was always standing between her and the cops, and Brunelle, like one of those room-dividing curtains in a hospital room. Present for the right intentions, but ultimately just annoying and ineffectual.

Nicholson finally arrived at 11:10, which seemed early to Brunelle because he had fully expected 11:20 to be the soonest they would see him.

"Dave!" Nicholson called out as the receptionist led them back into the conference room for a second time. "Detective Chan! Great to see you again. Sorry I'm late." He held up his phone. "New business, am I right?"

"Chen," the detective corrected, but Nicholson didn't seem to notice.

"So, we ready to do this?" Nicholson threw out his arms. "Again? I mean, like, really do this? Huh?"

Brunelle raised a single eyebrow but otherwise didn't move from his seat at the conference table. "We better be. There won't be a third chance. We need the entire story, and we need it now. And Nick?"

"Yes, Dave?"

"We need it without interruptions," Brunelle finished.

He had meant Nick interjecting himself between their questions and Sommers's answers. But apparently Nicholson hadn't even planned on doing that. He patted his phone. "No worries. I put it on silent."

"Fantastic," Brunelle replied. He turned to Chen. "Go ahead and start the recording."

Chen obliged and again recited the date, time, and names of those assembled. Last time, he had done the questioning. This time, Brunelle took the lead. Charges had been filed. It was his case now.

"Let's start with some background," Brunelle began. "I need you to explain to me, very specifically and exactly, your relationships with both Matt and Charlie Rycroft."

That wasn't directly part of the alibi, but it informed it. The believability of her story was directly related to the characters therein. Who was she trying to protect? Most likely, she was the same as anyone else: she was trying to protect herself.

Sommers sighed heavily. She frowned. She looked at Nicholson, who was looking at his phone. She looked back to

Brunelle and sighed again.

"I dated Matt for like two years," she made it sound like a confession. "We matched on some app and had drinks and we hit it off. It was supposed to be just for fun, but he can be a pretty intense guy. I guess I liked how much he liked me. So, it went from casual to serious to exclusive pretty quick. And he really wanted to get married. He kept talking about how smart and pretty our babies would be. Honestly, it was kind of gross. I wasn't looking to make babies with anyone. I'm still not. But he had this whole future planned out and he kept pressing me and eventually I guess he asked me to marry him, and I guess I said yes, and so then we were engaged or whatever."

I guess, whatever, Brunelle thought sarcastically. Still, there was something in the exasperation in her voice that made him believe her, even with all the hedging and verbal tics.

"But it was never like engaged-engaged, you know?" Sommers continued. She pulled painted nails through her long blond hair. "Like, we didn't ever pick a date or reserve a church or whatever. I just kind of agreed to it in principle and then he started going around telling everyone. Actually, I think that's kind of why I broke up with him eventually. He seemed way more interested in being engaged than in me as a person. And like I said, he was the one who was super into the commitment thing, so it wasn't really that hard for me to just do something to end it."

"What did you do?" Brunelle asked.

"I fucked his brother," Sommers responded, deadpan. "I mean, that did it, right? Like anything less than that and he would have been all, 'I forgive you' and 'We can work it out' and 'What color should the invitations be?' And I just wasn't looking for that. Plus, Charlie was cool, and kinda hot, so yeah."

She shrugged. "That's what happened."

Wow, Brunelle thought, but he didn't give voice to it. Instead, he kept his poker face and pressed ahead. "When did that all occur?"

Sommers frowned in thought and exhaled for a few seconds. "I dunno. Like three months ago? Four, maybe? I'm not sure."

"And then you started dating Charlie?" Brunelle followed up.

Another shrug. "Yeah, I guess. But I told him, nothing serious. I wasn't looking for serious. I'd just done serious and that's why I hooked up with him. Also, not exclusive. I wasn't looking for that either."

"So, you were dating other people?" Brunelle asked.

"Not really," Sommers answered. "Not yet. But I wanted to be able to, in case I wanted to start seeing someone else again."

"Like Matt?" Brunelle suggested.

Sommers chuckled and nodded. "Yeah, like Matt. I mean, once we weren't engaged anymore, I kinda was into him again. Charlie was cute or whatever, but Matt's hot. He's like an outdoorsman, with thick arms and he likes to lift heavy shit and just be like a man, you know?"

"And make babies," Brunelle said.

"Ugh, yeah," Sommers grimaced. "Don't remind me."

"When did you start up with Matt again?" Brunelle asked. "How long ago?"

"Not that long," Sommers put on a thoughtful expression. "I mean, less than a month, definitely. We only hooked up a couple of times."

"Did you tell Charlie?"

"I was going to," Sommers insisted, "but I didn't get the chance, because, well, he's dead."

Murdered, Brunelle thought, ever the prosecutor.

"So, the night that happened," Brunelle took the opportunity to segue, "you were with Matt, is that right?"

"For part of the night," Sommers answered. "Like I told you last time, he came over, but after we boned, he snuck out."

Brunelle just nodded. He would have to talk her to about vocabulary choice before she told her story to the jury. "Go on."

"Well, I guess he thought I was asleep," Sommers posited. "He got up, and I thought he was just going to the bathroom, but then I heard the front door open and close. I got up and sure enough, he was gone."

"What time was that?" Brunelle asked. That was key.

"Like ten o'clock?" Sommers estimated. "Right around then."

Perfect. Brunelle smiled.

"Did you see him drive away?" he asked. Maybe she could confirm the direction he went. Toward his brother's apartment, Brunelle hoped.

"Nah, you can't see the street from my apartment," she said. Brunelle recalled their visit to her building and supposed that was probably true. "Besides," she continued, "fuck him. If he wanted to sneak out on me and hook up with someone else, that's his business. I didn't want anything serious, right? Didn't bother me."

It seemed to bother her at the last interview, Brunelle recalled.

"It never occurred to me that he was going to go murder his brother," Sommers finished.

"Are you worth murdering someone over?" Chen

interjected. It was hardly a 'just the facts, ma'am' question, but Brunelle found himself interested in her response.

She looked to Nicholson again, who had at least stopped looking at his phone, for that moment anyway. He took a second, then nodded his head and rolled his wrist at her, communicating that she should answer the question.

She took a beat, then shrugged. "I guess so."

And Brunelle had to admit, that was the best possible answer. Looking at her, the jury would believe it.

"Are you done?" Chen abruptly asked Brunelle.

"Um," Brunelle had to take a moment. "I mean, maybe? I guess so. Why, do you--?"

"You and Matt were at your apartment in Seattle, correct?" Chen asked Sommers. "Not his house in Bellevue, right?"

"Uh, right," Sommers agreed.

"What time did you arrive?"

"At my own home?" Sommers questioned. "That's a weird way to phrase it."

"Did you work that day?" Chen asked with a roll of the eyes.

"Well, yes," Sommers admitted.

"What time did you arrive home?" Chen repeated.

"Um, I don't know. Like six-thirty, I guess," Sommers answered.

"What time did Matt arrive?"

"Like eight? Eight-thirty? Maybe later. I'm not a hundred percent."

"When did he leave?"

"Um, I'm not sure exactly," Sommers said. "It was after we, uh, well, after we boned. But we didn't stay up late really, so maybe eleven, eleven-thirty?"

11:00 in Roosevelt. Brunelle did the math in his head. Matt definitely could have made it to South Lake Union in time to commit the murder.

"Two more questions," Chen wrapped up. "What's your cell number? And what's Matt's?"

Sommers's eyebrows shot up. She looked again to Nicholson. He looked up from his phone and gave her another wrist roll. "Go ahead."

Sommers sighed, then took out her phone and unlocked it. "I don't know his number by heart or anything. He's just in my contacts, you know?"

"I know," Chen answered. He pulled out the small notepad he always kept in his jacket pocket, tore off a sheet, and slid it to Sommers, along with the pen that always accompanied the notepad. "Write it down, and yours."

Sommers frowned again. But she did as instructed.

When she slid the paper back to Chen, he stood up and tucked the phone numbers into his pocket.

"Are we done?" Brunelle wondered aloud.

Chen looked down at him and shrugged. "I am."

CHAPTER 16

"Call records," Brunelle said. "Of course."

"Not call records, Dave," Emory corrected him. "Phone records. GPS and cell tower pings. I don't care who they called—well, I do care about that actually, but it wasn't very interesting. What matters was where Rycroft's and Crossero's phones were."

"And Katie Sommers's," Brunelle realized.

"I didn't do anything about Katie Sommers's phone," Emory said. "She's the girlfriend, right?"

"Right," Brunelle confirmed. "Don't worry. You weren't working on her story. Chen is doing that. That's why he wanted her phone number."

"You pitted me and Larry against each other?" Emory asked. Then, before Brunelle could defend himself, she nodded approvingly. "Nice."

They were out to dinner. A local Asian food place that seemed like it was trying to be Vietnamese but had a lot of Thai and Chinese on the menu, plus sushi. In any event, it was good, cheap, and usually busy but not too busy. They'd easily found a table after ordering their combo meals and filling their plastic drinking glasses at the soda dispenser.

"It was more of a divide and conquer thing," Brunelle claimed. "I actually asked Chen to do both, but he said you had to do the Crossero story because it happened in Bellevue. Well, allegedly happened in Bellevue anyway."

"He's right," Emory replied over a sip of Coke. "Well, we didn't absolutely have to do it, but it would be irritating to have Seattle cops just coming into our city and asking questions. He wouldn't want us doing that to him either. You ever walk into a random courthouse in, I don't know, Pierce County and start prosecuting a case?"

"Just that once," Brunelle answered, glancing over his shoulder to see if the food was coming yet. It wasn't. He pushed the subject back to the current investigation. "So, what did you find out? What did you do?"

"First thing I did was interview James Crossero," Emory answered. "That declaration Rycroft's attorney typed up is worth less than nothing in my book. A lawyer could draft up anything and then just say 'sign it' at the bottom. I wanted to hear it directly from the witness."

"Smart," Brunelle responded. "I don't trust lawyers either. So, what did Crossero say?"

Emory laughed. "Pretty much exactly what he said in that declaration. He and Rycroft are buddies at work. They found out they're both playing the same MMO—"

"MMO?" Brunelle had to interrupt.

"Massively multiplayer online game," Emory translated. "It's a computer game where people from all over the world log on at the same time and play. Like Worlds of Warcraft."

Brunelle frowned and shook his head.

"Guild Wars?"

Another shake of the head.

Emory rolled her eyes. "Well, anyway, they were both huge nerds for this one game. I forget the name right now, but they set up a time for Crossero to come over to Rycroft's, load up on Mountain Dew and Doritos, and defeat evil hordes all night or whatever."

"Do these guys have girlfriends?" Brunelle tried a joke.

"Isn't that your theory of the case, counselor?" Emory turned it back on him. "Rycroft was heartbroken over his fiancée leaving him, so he murdered his brother out of jealousy?"

"Something like that." Brunelle shrugged. "I guess I heard he's hot. I don't know."

Emory shrugged too. "I'm not sure about Rycroft, but Crossero was pretty easy on the eyes."

Brunelle dropped his hand open. "Really? You're gonna tell your boyfriend that some criminal is sexy?"

"He's not a criminal, remember?" Emory responded. "He's the alibi witness."

"If he lied to you, he's a criminal," Brunelle retorted. "And I'm pretty sure he lied to you. He wasn't with Rycroft all night. Rycroft was with Katie Sommers. And Katie Sommers is pretty darn hot too, let me tell you."

Emory frowned. "Are you okay, Dave? That was," she sought the right word, "weird."

Brunelle frowned too. "Yeah, I guess it was. I don't know. I just don't like hearing you say some young tech guy is hot."

"I said he was easy on the eyes," Emory corrected, "and he's not a techie. He works at P.N.W. Outfitters. He's an outdoorsman."

"That's worse," Brunelle said.

"I know," Emory laughed. "Oh, cheer up. You're my guy, Dave. In fact, weren't we going to talk about that?"

"Uh, oh, yeah. Um, sure," Brunelle staggered through his response. "But why don't you tell me more about the investigation? Your investigation. Please tell me more about your investigation."

Emory grinned and shook her head. "Fine. But you're not getting out of here without at least talking about talking about it. I'm getting a little tired of just driving home the next morning because I'm going to get a parking ticket if I don't move my car."

"Understood." Brunelle craned his neck again for the food. Still no sign of it. He could always refill his drink if he needed a distraction. "So, what did you conclude from your investigation? Rycroft's alibi is shit, right?"

"Rycroft's alibi," Emory raised her glass, "is solid. He was in Bellevue all night."

Brunelle's shoulders dropped. "Are you fucking kidding me?"

"I am doing neither of those things, good sir," Emory responded. "Crossero was credible and consistent in his statement, but more importantly, I got the GPS information for his phone and Rycroft's. Rycroft got home around seven p.m. and never left. Crossero got there about thirty minutes later, same story. They were both inside that house all night."

Brunelle's gut twisted around itself. "Are you sure?"

"One hundred percent sure," Emory confirmed.

Brunelle's face contorted. "Well, that doesn't prove anything," he insisted. "It doesn't mean Rycroft was there all night. It just means his phone was."

"Who isn't with their phone twenty-four/seven these days, Dave?" Emory challenged.

"Well, maybe he wanted people to think he was there," Brunelle tried. "Maybe he knew you'd pull his phone records, so he left it there on purpose."

Emory sighed. "I suppose that's not impossible," she conceded.

"Sure, it's possible," Brunelle kept going. "Probably even likely. Wasn't he kind of cheating with his ex-fiancée? And what's that thing cheaters do? Two phones, two wallets, two sets of keys?"

Emory cocked her head at him. "What are you talking about?"

"If you're having an affair," Brunelle explained, "you have two phones so she can't read your text messages, two wallets so she can't read your credit card statements, and two sets of keys, I guess because you have a separate place or something for, well, you know."

Emory's brow furrowed. She crossed her arms. "Should I be worried that you know this?"

"What? Oh, no." Brunelle waved the suggestion away. "It's just one of those things you hear along the way and remember because it's kind of interesting."

"Okay," Emory allowed, "but why is it interesting?"

Brunelle got flustered. "I don't know. It's like those Secret Service guys who would cheat on their wives on every trip. Their motto was, 'wheels up, rings off'."

"Seriously, Dave, what the fuck?" Emory's initially playful scowl was hardened into a real one. "You saying all of this is not helping me want to have that other conversation right now." Her eyebrows shot up, to match the light bulb that could have appeared over her head. "Is that what you're doing? Are you doing this on purpose?"

Brunelle took a moment before responding. He finally noticed that she seemed actually upset. He'd upset women in the past, more often than he would have liked to admit, and for reasons he would have wanted even less to admit. He did not want to upset Casey Emory, and that had definitely not been his intention. He was talking without thinking. So, he needed to talk without overthinking. "I'm sorry." A good start. "I'm an idiot sometimes." True enough, they both knew. "I was thinking about our case, not about us. I want a reason to disbelieve Crossero and I was grasping. I could have handled that better. I didn't mean anything by it. And I'm sorry." Never hurts to say that twice.

Emory's expression relaxed, and then melted into an exasperated frown. An expression Brunelle was more than familiar with, and from more women than her. "You are an idiot sometimes," she agreed. "Lucky for you. It makes it easy to believe you didn't mean to make me upset. And even easier to believe you don't even know the real reason I'm upset."

Brunelle's eyebrows knitted together. Didn't she just say what was making her upset? But, idiot or not, he knew not to say that.

"It's not that you're disrespecting me as a girlfriend," Emory explained, "which you are, by the way. It's that you're disrespecting me as a detective."

Oh, Brunelle thought, *shit*.

"I told you I interviewed Crossero," Emory continued. "I told you he was credible and his story checked out. I told you I verified it with outside information. And instead of believing me, you reach back for some crazy cheating husband advice to tell me that you don't respect the work I did or the conclusions I drew."

Wow, he thought. "That's not what I meant."

"Maybe not," Emory replied, "but it's what you did."

An awkward silence hung over their table for several moments until the waiter arrived with their orders. Brunelle had lost his appetite. He picked up a fork and poked at the food. Then he frowned and looked up again at Emory. "I'm sorry."

"I know," Emory replied without looking at him. "But you're still going to pursue that secret other phone angle, aren't you?"

Brunelle sighed. She knew he wouldn't lie to her. Not right then anyway. "Yes."

CHAPTER 17

Chen had followed the same tactics. That's why he'd wanted Rycroft's and Sommers's phone numbers. He confirmed with Brunelle that Rycroft's phone was in Bellevue the entire night, and Sommers's never left her apartment in Roosevelt. And that just confirmed in Brunelle's mind that Rycroft's alibi was too good to be true.

"So, what's his other phone number?" Brunelle demanded of Amanda West as soon as he walked up to her at their next court date. This one was what they called an 'omnibus hearing'. It was like the pretrial conference, inasmuch as it wasn't a formal hearing in front of a judge with witnesses and evidence and arguments and rulings. It was designed to bring the two attorneys together to discuss the case off the record and see whether the case couldn't resolve short of trial, like the other 95% of criminal cases did. And if the case wasn't going to resolve, they would fill out a form outlining everything—hence 'omnibus'—that needed to be completed and when to make sure the parties were ready for trial on the assigned trial date.

"I beg your pardon?" West responded. She was standing

in the crowd, not having found a seat yet. "His other phone number? What are you talking about?"

"I'm talking about the burner phone he took with him when he left Katie Sommers's bed," Brunelle declared, "and drove ten minutes to his brother's apartment to murder his rival for the fair Ms. Sommers's affections."

West blinked at him for several seconds. "The fair Ms. Sommers?" she repeated. "Are you commenting on her attractiveness? Is that why your judgment is so skewed on this?"

That struck a nerve. He jabbed a finger at her. "That is not why my judgment is askew." Then he thought for a moment and corrected himself. "My judgment is not askew. Or skewed. Or whatever you said. My judgment is fine. I can see what really happened and I can see how it happened. I'll take good, old-fashioned eyewitness testimony over tech gadgets and GPS locations."

West nodded. "So, James Crossero's statement checked out, I take it. Good. Will I be getting a written police report on that, or were you planning on sweeping that part of your investigation under the rug?"

That was an insult too far. Brunelle's finger jabbed the air again. "I don't hide information. Ever. If I wanted to do that, I wouldn't have started this conversation by bringing it up in the first place."

West didn't have a response ready for that.

"But I'm not worried," Brunelle continued. "The murder was like a personal signature, and the weapon links your client to it. The means was that Swiss Army knife. The motive was Katie Sommers, fair or lovely or whatever."

"Oh, so now she's lovely," West noted. "What about

opportunity, Monsieur Poirot? Isn't that kind of the entire point of an alibi? To show that the suspect didn't have the opportunity to commit the crime?"

"Exactly, Dr. Watson," Brunelle responded. "If you can't escape your motive, and the means leads directly to you, then the only thing you can do is lie and claim you didn't have the opportunity."

West took a beat. "You know Watson was Sherlock Holmes's sidekick, right? Poirot's was Colonel Hastings."

Brunelle's lips tightened a bit and he shook his head. "I don't know who that is."

"Obviously," West sighed. "So, look, I'm sensing that you're having an adversarial relationship with reality right now, and you know what? That's fine. That's your thing, and I'm going to go ahead and wish you well. In the meantime, though, I have a job to do."

At that, she pulled a document out of her case file and handed it to Brunelle. He read the caption aloud. "Defendant's Motion to Dismiss for Insufficient Evidence." He looked up at her. "Isn't that kind of the jury's decision?"

"Not if there's no way any reasonable jury could conclude my client committed the crime," West returned. "When that's the case, the judge should dismiss it before trial."

"Because it's a waste of judicial resources," Brunelle finished her sentence with the usual argument for those types of motions.

"No," West answered. "Because it's morally and ethically wrong to put a defendant through a criminal trial and subject them to possible loss of liberty should the jury believe the siren songs of the prosecution when even the judge knows there is insufficient evidence to support the charges."

Brunelle pursed his lips. "Well, yeah, that too."

"So, you agree?" West asked hopefully.

"That innocent people shouldn't have to go through a trial? Definitely," Brunelle answered. "That your client is one of those innocent people? Definitely not."

West sighed again and shook her head.

"File your motion," Brunelle said. "I'll file my response. Then I'll win the motion and we will do that trial after all."

West paused again before replying. "I guess I am new at this, but I'm really not one for all this trash talking. I'll let my brief do the talking."

Brunelle had to respect that. But trash talking was also part of the fun.

"I guess I can do that too," he tried to lower the temperature. "So, shall we advise the Court that we need a hearing date prior to the trial date?"

"I think that is the appropriate thing to do," West answered. They started walking toward the courtroom and West held up the form the judges required the attorneys to fill out at the omnibus hearing. "And we can file this. I went ahead and filled most of it out."

"Thank you," Brunelle responded.

"I even checked the box," West continued with a grin, "for 'Defense will kick prosecution's ass'."

Brunelle smiled as well. The trash talking was definitely fun.

CHAPTER 18

Brunelle wasn't a huge fan of writing briefs. He preferred the courtroom to his office. The drama and performance of live testimony, rapid objections, and arguments built by logic and fueled by passion. But he didn't mind drafting the response to West's motion to dismiss too much. She may have had some facts on her side—like a witness who would swear Rycroft was with him the night of the murder—but the law was entirely against her.

"What are you working on?" Emory sat down on the couch next to him, drinks in hand, and glanced at his laptop screen.

Brunelle's instinct was to turn it away from her, but he managed to resist. The last thing he wanted to talk about was the last thing they talked about: him not believing her investigation.

"Work," he tried. "You know, lawyer stuff. Annoying."

"Um-hmm," Emory agreed. She set Brunelle's drink on his coffee table and leaned back into his soft couch. It would be another early morning of moving her car before she got ticketed.

"Are you going to win?"

"Yes," Brunelle was quick to reply. "I mean, I should. The law is pretty clear."

"What's the issue?" Emory took a sip from her drink, hot apple cider laced with bourbon.

"Uh," Brunelle hesitated. "It's just a motion to dismiss for lack of evidence, but, um, you know, as long as I have any evidence at all, then really the case should go to the jury."

"Makes sense." Emory took another sip. "Is there going to be an actual hearing, like in front of a judge?"

Brunelle nodded. "Yeah, in a couple of weeks."

"Witnesses?"

"No, just legal argument," Brunelle answered. "That's kind of the point of the motion."

"Well, that's good," Emory remarked.

"Why is that?" Brunelle wondered aloud.

"Can you imagine," Emory shook her head, "your girlfriend testifying against you like that?"

Brunelle's heart skipped a beat. He hadn't thought of that.

"I guess," Emory laughed, "we'll just have to wait until the trial."

CHAPTER 19

The hearing on West's motion to dismiss was set exactly two weeks after she filed her pleadings at the omnibus and exactly two weeks before the trial was scheduled to start. If she won, the trial date would be stricken, the case would be dismissed, and Matthew Rycroft would walk out of jail a free man.

But she wasn't going to win.

Probably.

Brunelle was pretty sure she would lose.

The law said she should lose. But, he had to admit, the facts kind of suggested she should win.

He frowned as he set his things down on the prosecution table inside the courtroom where the hearing would be held. He wasn't one for arriving early, although he wasn't one to be late either. He was one for arriving on time, if at all possible. Late was awkward, and early meant small talk. But that morning he had been earlier than he wanted. Probably just nerves, he told himself. Until he asked himself why he was nervous if he was supposed to win so easily.

The motion had been assigned to judge Jonathan Richter, which meant Richter was the betting favorite to be the trial judge too. In theory, it could be any of the county's 51 judges, but once one of them heard a pretrial motion, especially one that required the judge to become familiar with literally all of the evidence in the case, it was likely the case would stay with them for trial as well. The judges had enough to do—too much, just like everyone else in the criminal justice system. It would have been a waste of resources to have two judges learn all the facts of one case.

The case of *The State of Washington versus Matthew Rycroft*. One count of murder in the first degree. Brunelle represented the good people of the great State of Washington. And the defendant was represented by...

"Amanda West," she had to tell the bailiff her name when she arrived because she had never set foot in Judge Richter's courtroom before.

"Are you ready for your client, Ms., uh, West?" the bailiff asked.

West took a moment to scan the courtroom in order to assess the question. It was empty save her, the bailiff, and Brunelle. Obviously, she would need her client...

"I'll call the jail," the bailiff explained, "and the guards will transport him to the courtroom."

Unlike the presiding courtroom where in-custody criminal matters were heard all day, every day, and therefore holding cells and a secure hallway to the jail had been built behind the courtroom, Judge Richter's room was just another courtroom at the end of another long marble hallway of courtrooms, none of which were so singularly dedicated to jailed defendants as to justify the expense of doing more than having two guards march a handcuffed defendant down the regular hallways, one to yell at the congregating lawyers, clients, and witnesses to get out of the way and the other to keep an eye on Matthew Rycroft as he was perp-walked into Judge Richter's courtroom.

"I'll give you a moment with your client," the bailiff said. "Judge Richter will be taking the bench shortly."

Richter was like that. He gave the lawyers a little bit of latitude, but not too much. He'd been a trial attorney himself for the better part of twenty years before he got appointed to finish the term of one of the old timers who passed away before he got the chance to retire. Richter was well enough known, and well enough respected, and well enough feared, that no one ran against him when the term ended, or at any of the other elections since then.

His little way of saying thanks was to take the bench about five minutes late, to allow everyone to settle in before having to turn it on. He never let court go past noon, and he actually read all of the briefs that were filed by the lawyers who appeared in front of him. That last part shouldn't have been rare, but it was, and increasingly so, or at least that's how it felt to Brunelle as the average age of the judges transformed from decades older than him, to the same age, to a steadily increasing number of years younger.

Maybe Richter had the right idea. Get out of the day-to-day practice of law before it took you out. But Brunelle knew he'd miss playing the game if he gave it up to become one of the referees. The only real perk of being a judge seemed to be that everyone stood up when you entered the courtroom and the bailiff called out:

"All rise! The King County Superior Court is now in

session, The Honorable Jonathan Richter presiding."

Richter took the bench and gazed down amicably at the parties assembled before him. His hair was thin and black and graying at the temples, and his face was clean-shaven with skin that was wrinkled and tanned, but from outdoor activities so it seemed healthy somehow. His eyes were sharp and focused.

"Are the parties ready on the matter of *The State of Washington versus Matthew Rycroft?*"

Brunelle, still standing from the initial call to rise, responded first. "The State is ready, Your Honor."

"The defense is also ready, Your Honor," West confirmed, also still standing, Rycroft had sat down after the judge came out, then tried to stand up again, but couldn't quite because of the awkwardness of the leg chains binding his ankles together.

"Good," Richter said. "Then let's get started, shall we? This is a defense motion to dismiss, correct, Ms. West? I believe the caption of your brief said, 'motion to dismiss for insufficient evidence', or words to that effect, but do we all agree this is a *Knapstad* motion?"

State v. Knapstad was the Washington Supreme Court case that expanded the civil practice of moving to dismiss for failure to state a claim into the criminal realm. In civil practice, when a plaintiff was just suing for money, if what they were complaining about was something you can't get money for, then the judge could throw the case out long before it got anywhere close to a jury. It was such a problem, and so common of one, that they put it right into the civil court rules. As a result, those motions were called '12(b)(6) motions' after the relevant rule. But there was no such criminal court rule. So, in theory, a prosecutor could charge anyone with anything, whether there was any evidence or not, and force a defendant to sit through a trial, scared to death of going to prison, even if there weren't actually any facts to support the charge. Prosecutors weren't supposed to do that. They were supposed to have higher ethics. That's probably why they didn't think they needed to write a court rule against all that. But not all prosecutors did have higher ethics, and that's why the Washington Supreme Court had to craft the rule into case law several decades earlier when some prosecutor's office insisted on prosecuting a Ms. Knapstad for a crime she very clearly did not commit. Her husband clearly did commit the crime, by the way, and that seemed to be the reason for prosecuting Ms. Knapstad as well, as a sort of bargaining chip. That probably didn't impress the State Supreme Court either.

So, after that case, criminal defendants could file the functional equivalent of a 12(b)(6) motion and everyone who practiced criminal law called them '*Knapstad* motions'. Amanda West's failure to do so just underlined her lack of experience and general in-over-her-headedness.

"Yes, Your Honor," Brunelle responded. "I believe this is a *Knapstad* motion, and I drafted my response accordingly."

"Um, yes, Your Honor," West agreed cautiously. Brunelle enjoyed watching her walk the tightrope of acknowledging she didn't know the jargon without letting her client know she didn't know the jargon. "I believe I cited to that case in my brief, of course. I just didn't include the name of the case in my caption."

Brunelle frowned in approval. *Pretty good tightrope walk.* It probably helped that Rycroft had no idea what they were talking about.

"All right then. I'm glad we're agreed," Judge Richter

said. "That means it's the defense's motion and I will hear first from the defense. Ms. West, whenever you're ready."

Brunelle sat down again, a bit intrigued by Richter's decision to hear West's argument first. He was correct that it was a defense motion, but it was a defense motion challenging the sufficiency of the State's evidence. Usually, that meant the prosecution went first. If the prosecutor couldn't meet their burden, then there was literally no need to hear from the defense; the defense won.

So, either Richter had already decided how he was going to rule, or he was testing to see whether West knew she should insist Brunelle go first. Maybe both. Probably both. Either way, Brunelle could relax a bit and scout West's oral advocacy skills in advance of the trial.

"Thank you, Your Honor." West remained standing to deliver her argument. A lawyer always stands up when addressing the judge. At least she knew that much. "As the Court is aware, but to state for the record regardless, my client, Mr. Matthew Rycroft, has been charged by the State of Washington, and the prosecutor Mr. Brunelle specifically, with one count of the crime of murder in the first degree."

That was a lot of words, Brunelle thought, for something that was already pretty clearly in the record the moment Brunelle filed the complaint at the arraignment.

"In order to prove, beyond a reasonable doubt, that my client committed that murder," West continued, "the State will need to put on evidence that Mr. Rycroft was the one who actually did the acts that caused the death of his dear, beloved brother, Charles Rycroft."

Again, Brunelle thought, pretty elementary stuff so far. He wasn't impressed. But he was starting to feel relieved if this was how she was going to be in the trial.

"Go on," Richter interjected. It sounded encouraging. It wasn't. What he really meant was, 'Move on'.

"Yes, thank you, Your Honor," West responded.

Brunelle wondered if she understood the judge's true meaning. But then again, he didn't suppose it mattered much.

"So, in order to prove that," West continued, "they need to prove he was actually there, present in the victim's apartment, at the moment the victim was murdered. I know that seems very basic, Your Honor, but there's a reason it seems very basic, and that's because it is very basic."

Basically. Brunelle grinned slightly to himself.

"And it is that very basic piece of the case," West continued, "which the prosecution simply will not be able to prove. The reason they will not be able to prove it is that Mr. Rycroft, Mr. *Matthew* Rycroft, was not present when his brother was murdered. Indeed, he wasn't even in the same city. While someone, we know not who except we know that it was not my client—someone was in Charles Rycroft's Seattle apartment, murdering him, my client was on the other side of Lake Washington, in Bellevue, nowhere near or in any way involved in that murder, and we have a witness to prove it."

Judge Richter frowned at that. He frowned for the same reason Brunelle was smiling. Brunelle wondered whether Richter would interrupt West and try to direct her to the proper inquiry.

"An alibi witness?" Judge Richter inquired.

"Yes, Your Honor, exactly," West confirmed. "A young man by the name of James Crossero, who will testify that my client was with him all night in Bellevue and therefore could not have committed the murder."

Richter nodded. "I believe you attached his written statement to your brief as an exhibit, isn't that right?"

"That is correct, Your Honor," West agreed. "That is what Mr. Crossero will testify to at trial."

"And you'll be the one calling him as a witness, I presume?" Richter asked. "Not Mr. Brunelle?"

"Uh, well, I don't want to speak for Mr. Brunelle," West hesitated.

Brunelle didn't hesitate. He stood up. "The State will absolutely not be calling Mr. Crossero in its case-in-chief, Your Honor."

That may have seemed a bit smarmy, but it was actually vital to the determination of the motion.

"Okay, I think I understand your argument, Ms. West," Richter said. "Perhaps I should hear from Mr. Brunelle now?"

West frowned. "Will I be afforded an opportunity to respond, Your Honor?"

"Of course," the judge assured her. "It's your motion. You get the final word. I don't want Mr. Brunelle to think he can make arguments with impunity."

Richter grinned at Brunelle, and Brunelle could only smile back. He wasn't planning on making any inappropriate arguments. Just winning ones.

"Whenever you're ready, Mr. Brunelle," Richter invited him.

"Thank you, Your Honor. As much as I enjoyed hearing the preview of Ms. West's closing argument, I do believe it was premature. We aren't here to determine whether the defendant committed the crime, although obviously the State believes he did. That is for a jury to determine. The question before the Court today, and the only question before the Court today, is whether a jury will be allowed to determine that. Whether this Court should take away the jury's right to decide this case. And the Court can only do that if the Court does really do that, if the Court decides there is absolutely no jury, ever, anywhere at all, that could possibly, under any circumstances, find the defendant guilty."

Brunelle took a moment to assess if Judge Richter was picking up what Brunelle was putting down. Richter gave him a nod to confirm that he understood.

"And when making that decision," Brunelle continued, "the Court doesn't weigh the evidence. The Court doesn't listen to the defense's closing argument and decide whether the State has proven its case. No. The Court assumes all of the State's evidence is true, draws any and all reasonable inference in favor of the State, and ignores any evidence the defense may or may not plan to present at trial. That, Your Honor, is the legal standard today. This is a challenge to the sufficiency of the State's evidence, and so the only evidence to consider is that evidence, and none other."

Brunelle gestured toward West, who was for some unknown reason still standing as Brunelle spoke. At least Rycroft was sitting down.

"That is why it is important to note," Brunelle continued, "that the State will not be introducing any of defendant's alleged alibi defense through Mr. James Crossero or any other witness. That is not a part of the State's evidence, and as such it cannot be considered by the Court today when ruling on this motion. Put another way, the defense can't argue that the State has insufficient evidence because they have evidence too. If there's competing evidence, then the jury decides, and that is exactly what the Court should allow to happen here."

Brunelle turned his full attention back to the judge, but couldn't help but notice West still standing out of the corner of his eye. It was distracting. Luckily, he was almost done.

"So, then, what evidence does the State have?" Brunelle posed the question. "Well, Your Honor, the State has the dead body of Charles Rycroft. The State has the expert opinion of the medical examiner that the manner of death was homicide. We further have his expert opinion that the wounds were created by several different weapons, all of which are typically collected together into a single tool commonly known as a Swiss Army knife. We have the fact that the defendant works for an outdoor recreation company that sells exactly that sort of tool. We have a motive to kill inasmuch as the victim had stolen away the defendant's fiancée."

Lovely fiancée, his brain couldn't stop from thinking.

"And, we have testimony from that fiancée that she was with the defendant earlier on the night of the murder, but then the defendant sneaked out and was gone at the exact time the murder occurred. Oh, and when confronted by law enforcement about where he was that night, and whether he in fact had an alibi, the defendant said, 'No'."

Brunelle couldn't help but throw a truly smarmy grin at West. Her eyes were fixed on the judge.

"That is the State's evidence, Your Honor," Brunelle turned back to Richter. "That is the evidence this Court must consider today, and only that evidence. And that evidence is absolutely sufficient to allow this case to proceed to trial so that a jury may decide the defendant's fate. Thank you."

Judge Richter nodded again, then turned back to West. "I promised you the last word, Ms. West. Any reply?"

"As a matter of fact, no, Your Honor," West said, to

everyone's surprise, including her client's, if his expression was any sign. "I leave it to this learned Court to render an appropriate ruling." Then she finally sat down.

Richter cocked his head at her, but then nodded once again. Judges nodded a lot. They weren't really supposed to give away what they were thinking about any particular evidence or argument, especially in front of the jury, so they all got into the habit of just sort of nodding along. Brunelle remembered that and suddenly felt a little less secure about that whole picking up what he was putting down thing.

"First of all," Judge Richter began, "I'd like to thank both attorneys for the effort they brought to bear on this motion. The briefing in this case was really very good. Both lawyers provided me with not only thorough legal analysis, but ample exhibits to feel comfortable that I knew all of the facts that might be presented at trial, both in the State's case-in-chief and in the defense's case-in-chief, should the defendant elect to put on a case."

Brunelle smiled slightly. Everyone enjoyed being complimented. He could see why no one bothered to run against the guy who made everyone feel good about themselves.

"I think the determination of today's motion is controlled completely by the standard I am permitted to apply at this stage in the life of the case," Richter continued. "If I were being asked to weigh the evidence, compare and contrast it, decide what to believe and what to discard, well, then, that would be a trial, and I would of course endeavor to render a proper verdict. But today is not the trial. Today is a motion to dismiss upon a claim that the evidence could never ever produce a guilty verdict—a claim that if the case were tried a thousand times, then the verdict would be, one thousand times, not guilty. And I agree with Mr. Brunelle that in so deciding that narrowly focused question, I am bound to consider only the State's evidence, and nothing which the defense may add to that evidence at trial."

Exactly, Brunelle thought. He felt better again about the ruling.

"I will take a moment here," Richter said, "to take note of the assurance by Mr. Brunelle that he will not be calling James Crossero in his case-in-chief. Because of that representation, I cannot and will not consider anything in the declaration of Mr. Crossero provided by Ms. West. As a result, there is no evidence before me today that the defendant has an alibi. Rather, the evidence is as Mr. Brunelle stated, and I certainly cannot say that no reasonable jury could possibly find the defendant guilty. He had the motive, the means, and—again, not considering Mr. Crossero's statement—the opportunity."

Brunelle couldn't help but throw another quick sideways glance at West. Not exactly 'I told you so' but not exactly not that either.

"Therefore," the judge concluded, "I find that the State is in possession of sufficient evidence to allow the case to proceed to a jury. Accordingly, I hereby deny the defendant's motion to dismiss for insufficient evidence."

Brunelle nodded and smiled, satisfied with himself. A final glance at West, but what he saw surprised him. She seemed to appear satisfied as well. He didn't necessarily need to see West deflated and defeated, but he wouldn't have minded it either. Instead, however, she wore a confident smile and patted her client reassuringly on the back as the guards stepped over to escort him back to his cell.

Brunelle stepped over to extend a hand in victory.

"Well argued, counsel," Brunelle offered. "Better luck next time. I mean, not too much luck, of course. But again, well argued."

West shook his hand, a solid grip, not held too long. "Thank you, Mr. Brunelle. I accomplished everything I think I could have today."

Brunelle frowned. He thought he had won the hearing. "Well, you didn't get the case dismissed," he pointed out.

West laughed. "I was never going to get the case dismissed. Everyone in this courtroom knew that. Well, maybe except my client, but you can hardly blame him for getting his hopes up, right?"

"Um, right," Brunelle supposed. "I guess."

"I mean, there's always a chance," West went on. "I could have gotten lucky, but what elected judge is going to throw out a murder case just because, I don't know, the defendant is innocent or something?"

Brunelle grimaced. "Agree to disagree on that point."

West laughed again. "Sure. But either way, I accomplished what I set out to do."

"And what was that exactly?" Brunelle asked. "If it wasn't to actually get the case dismissed."

"Well, for starters, I got to see how you are in court," West answered. "I need to scout my opposition. Another thing is that I also got to see the preview of your closing argument. Or at least your opening statement, when you won't mention James Crossero because you just promised the judge you wouldn't. And finally, I got that promise from you. The judge relied on your promise not to call Crossero, so you can't change your mind about that without risking the judge reconsidering his ruling and maybe actually dismissing the case after all. So, I know you won't call him first in your case-in-chief to try to discredit him in advance or 'draw the sting', as they say."

Brunelle found himself speechless. Another accomplishment by West that day.

"All in all, a good day's work." She smiled broadly and picked up her briefcase. "I guess I'll see you in two weeks, Mr. Brunelle. Oh, and you might want to work on that opening statement. It was kind of predictable."

With that West headed for the exit, and Brunelle headed for a panic.

CHAPTER 20

Chen narrowed his eyes as Brunelle's recitation. "So, it was all some brilliant strategy? I don't know. It sounds like she was just playing off a loss as a win. Don't all you lawyers do that?"

Brunelle considered for a moment. "I mean, yeah, we kinda do. But she wasn't wrong. I'm completely blocked from calling Crossero as a witness now in my case."

"Why would you call him in your case?" Chen asked. "He's their witness."

They were sitting in Chen's office in that hour between 5:00, when they say you can go home, and 6:00, when you really might have gotten enough work done to actually be able to go home. Brunelle needed to vent to someone, and Chen wasn't one to swing by the prosecutor's office unless he had to. He didn't have much use for lawyers, in truth. That was one, but only one, of the several reasons Brunelle didn't want to vent to Emory either.

Brunelle shrugged. "It's called 'drawing the sting'. Sometimes the other side has some pretty good evidence. If you wait and let them present it, it looks like you didn't know about it and got ambushed. It must be really important and really hurt your case. But if you bring it up first, it looks like you don't think it's that big of a deal. It takes away their 'A-ha!' moment, and you can manage, at least a little bit, how it's presented to the jury."

"Makes sense." Chen nodded. "And now you can't do it?"

"Nope."

"Because of what you told the judge?"

"Yup."

"So, that was pretty stupid, then, huh?"

Brunelle cocked his head at his friend. "I was trying to win the motion. Which I did, by the way."

"Sounds like you won the battle," Chen replied, "but she's setting up to win the war."

Brunelle crossed his arms and narrowed his own eyes. "Not if I can help it."

"What are you going to do?" Chen asked.

"I," Brunelle pointed a finger across the desk at his lead detective, "do not know."

CHAPTER 21

In the end, Brunelle did what lawyers do. He talked. Lawyers talk. And talk, and talk, and talk. That's the main skill set. Talking to juries, talking to judges, talking to clients, and witnesses, and opposing counsel. Even the written briefs were more talking, just in a different format. The better lawyers also knew stuff—law and evidence rules, etc.—but the level of knowledge of those sorts of things was uneven in the profession and not as closely correlated to success as an outsider might expect.

The question for Brunelle was whom to talk to. Not the professionals, he concluded. He'd already talked to Chen, for what that had been worth. He was avoiding talking to Emory, for more than one reason. He was avoiding Nicholson even more. And he wasn't going to gain anything by talking with West any further, at least not right then.

That left the civilians who were involved, but there were challenges there, too. Charles Rycroft was dead. Brunelle wasn't allowed to talk to Matthew Rycroft—that whole 'right to remain silent' thing. Talking to Sommers meant going through

Nicholson, so no. That left one person he could talk to without having to go through someone else and who could possibly help Brunelle piece his case back together before trial.

"I'm looking for James Crossero," Brunelle advised the first person he spotted in the P.N.W. Outfitters sales team uniform of dark green polo shirt and khaki pants. "Is he working today?"

If he'd had a badge, it would have been a good time to show it. Dispel any concerns the salesperson might have from some random stranger walking in off the street and asking for one of her coworkers. But he had a uniform of his own, and it had a similar effect. Dark suit, white shirt, vibrant tie. Short hair, clean-shaven, tall. White. Male. Old. *Well, old-er,* he told himself. He was obviously some sort of authority, not a crazy ex-boyfriend or Craigslist serial killer. The young saleswoman sized him up, nodded slightly, and responded.

"We don't share work schedules with the public. If there's something you want to buy, I can help you. Otherwise, the best we can do is give him your name and number and tell him you came in looking for him."

Brunelle frowned. That was not the response he was hoping for, or expecting.

"It's the suit, right?" he looked down at his ensemble and laughed at himself. "No one wears suits anymore, do they? Not even bankers. Maybe lawyers, if they're in court or something, I don't know. But no, I just came from a meeting with—well, it's not important—but I was in here a couple of days ago and James helped me pick out like a whole huge camping gear set. New everything, even a kayak. It was kind of a lot of money, but he's a really good salesman. So, I really want to make sure he gets the commission, you know?"

"We don't work on commission, sir," the young woman replied. "And James doesn't work in the camping department."

"What department does he work in?"

"I can give him your name and number, if you want," she repeated. Then she pointed toward the section of the store filled with tent displays. "Or you can go over to camping and talk to them about your impressively large purchase you didn't actually talk to James about."

Brunelle frowned. If he'd worn a hat with his suit, he would have tipped it to her. "Thank you, miss. I'll just be going then."

"You don't want to leave your name and number?" she offered one more time.

"No thanks," Brunelle answered. "I have other means of contacting him."

Once outside, Brunelle took out his phone and employed those other means.

"Hello. This is Chen."

"I need a photo of James Crossero," Brunelle half-whispered as he walked away from the P.N.W. building. "Like his driver's license photo or something. Can you get that and send it to me?"

"Dave?"

"Yes, it's Dave," Brunelle hissed. "Obviously, it's me."

"You're trying to track down Crossero?" Chen asked. "Why don't you just go to the store where he worked with Rycroft?"

"Yes, well, obviously because I don't have a badge," Brunelle answered. "Do you think they're just going to tell me when a certain employee is scheduled to work?"

"Not if you're weird about it," Chen said. "Oh. You

went, didn't you? And you were weird about it? Are you wearing a suit? No one wears suits anymore, Dave."

"Just send me the photo, okay?" Brunelle snapped. "I'll take care of the rest."

He could hear Chen chuckle over the phone. "Sure, Dave. Give me a few minutes and you can start your stakeout. There's probably a donut shop nearby. Or maybe more like vegan smoothies or something."

Brunelle didn't return the laugh, but did offer a curt "Thanks," then waited on the photo. It only took Chen about ten minutes. By then, Brunelle had his smoothie and took up a spot across the street from P.N.W. Outfitters to wait for James Crossero to leave work.

It took longer than Brunelle might have wanted. He didn't time his visit to coincide with their shift schedule, not that he knew when that was actually, but eventually a man matching the image and physicals on James Edward Crossero's driver's license—5'9", 210 pounds, black hair, brown eyes—emerged from the building across the street and Brunelle jumped up to head him off before he disappeared around the corner.

"Mr. Crossero! James Crossero!" Brunelle called out as he reached the other side of the street. "Mr. Crossero, I need to speak with you for a moment."

Crossero turned around to see who was calling his name. When he saw Brunelle jogging toward him, he shook his head. "Are you that weird old guy Caitlyn said was asking about me? She said you were wearing a suit."

Brunelle could hardly deny the suit he was wearing, but he wasn't ready to concede the rest of the description.

"I'm not weird," he insisted, already too out of breath to make the next denial credible, "and I'm not that old. But yeah, that was me. Do you have a few moments? My name is David Brunelle and I'm a prosecutor with the King County Prosecutor's Office. I wanted to talk to you about your friend, Matt Rycroft."

Crossero squinted at Brunelle. "You're the prosecutor? So, that means you want to put Matt in prison, right?"

Kinda, Brunelle thought, but he knew better than to admit that. "It means I'm trying to hold his brother Charlie's killer responsible. Right now, it looks like Matt is the killer, but I understand maybe he was with you that night, so I wanted to talk to you. I'm only interested in figuring out what really happened that night."

And winning. He was a little bit interested in winning. As long as winning was the just thing to do. He still thought it was. He doubted Crossero would change that, but he might help Brunelle confirm it, even if unwittingly.

Crossero frowned. He didn't seem convinced. "Well, if you really care about that truth," he said, "the truth is that Matt was with me all night. He couldn't have murdered his brother. I mean, he never would have, but also he couldn't have. I already told his lawyer that. Some lady. I figured she would have told you."

"She did," Brunelle advised. "That's why I'm here. Ms. West provided me with a typewritten statement you signed, but I had some questions about it that she really couldn't answer because it wasn't like she was playing M.M.O. with you that night too."

Crossero's face twisted into a puzzle knot.

"Did I say that wrong?" Brunelle asked. "M.M.O, like massive multiplayer o— um, organic video game? Is that right?"

Crossero winced. "No, man, that is not right."

"Well, whatever." Brunelle waved his own confusion to the side. "The point is, she wasn't with you guys that night so she can't really answer my questions."

"What questions?" Crossero challenged. "Matt was with me all night. What else is there to know?"

"Well, let's start there and define terms," Brunelle suggested. "What exactly do you mean by 'all night'?"

"I'm mean 'all night'," Crossero answered. "Like, the entire night."

"The whole night?" Brunelle challenged. "You were with him the entire time?"

"Yes."

"Every single minute?" Brunelle demanded. "Every second?"

"Yes."

"Did you go with him when he went to the bathroom?" Brunelle asked.

Crossero shifted his weight. "Well, no, obviously not."

"So, not every second then?" Brunelle observed.

"Okay, not every second," Crossero admitted.

"What about grabbing snacks?" Brunelle asked. "Did you two always go to the kitchen together? Did you hold hands maybe?"

Crossero narrowed his eyes again at Brunelle. "Are you being homophobic?"

"What? No!" Brunelle shook his head. Why were these young people so sensitive nowadays? "No, look, I'm just trying to make a point. You weren't actually with him every single second you were over there. It would be weird if you had been. That's not normal. You weren't with him every second, and you can't account for his every action that night. I mean, it's not like you knew a bunch of cops and lawyers would come asking you about it weeks later, right?"

"It was only a couple of days later," Crossero answered, "but yeah. I mean, I wasn't watching his every move or whatever, but I think I would have noticed if he'd gone and murdered somebody."

"Right?" Brunelle seemed to agree. "You would think you'd notice that. Unless, you didn't."

"He didn't murder anyone," Crossero said. "I'm sure of that."

"Are you sure he didn't murder his brother because you know he didn't leave?" Brunelle asked, "or are you sure he didn't leave because you know he wouldn't have murdered his brother?"

Crossero shook his head at that. "What does that even mean, man?"

"One more question," Brunelle said, "then I'll leave you alone."

"Okay, fine, whatever," Crossero responded.

"Did you sleep at all that night?" Brunelle asked. "Did Matt?"

"That's two questions, dude," Crossero pointed out with a grin.

"I could rephrase it," Brunelle proposed, "or you could just answer it. Did either of you sleep that night?"

Crossero shrugged. "I mean, sure. A little bit. But like, not a lot. That was the whole point, you know? My birthday was coming up, so it was like an early birthday party, you know? Just me and him. We were gonna stay up all night playing so I could level my character up for my birthday. But yeah, I mean, we're human. We both slept a little bit here and there."

Brunelle nodded, first as the answer came in, then to himself in thought.

"Thank you, Mr. Crossero," he said. "I appreciate your cooperation."

"So, like did I help Matt?" Crossero asked. "Are you going to drop the charges?"

"Did you tell the truth?" Brunelle countered.

"Yeah."

"Then you helped Matt," Brunelle answered. "But no, I'm not dropping the charges." He reached up for the brim of that old-timey hat he wasn't wearing. "Have a good day."

CHAPTER 22

Just because you're paranoid, doesn't mean they aren't after you.

That quote ran through Brunelle's mind as he stepped back from his Unabomber-like diagram that covered the large whiteboard on the wall opposite his desk. Photographs of the murder scene and the autopsy joined maps of Seattle and Bellevue and driver's license photos of Charlie Rycroft, Matt Rycroft, Katie Sommers, and James Crossero. Color-coded lines connected the players and locations, with approximate times of key events, and potential motives. But not motives for murder. Motives to lie.

There were really only a few motives to lie. The most common one, as verified by actual psychological studies about that sort of thing, was a desire to avoid punishment. Brunelle understood that. He made a living from that. And he was human too. All too human sometimes.

The other main motive to lie was a desire to get something the person didn't think they could otherwise get. Dating profiles came to mind. But he never really understood that. If the person actually cared about what you did for a living or where you went to school, they were going to find out the truth eventually. And if it was a one-night stand, did they really care about that stuff anyway? He supposed they must, at least some of them, or else people would stop doing it. Kids these days.

The last big motive to lie was the hardest one to tease out in a puzzle like the one strewn across his whiteboard. Some people just enjoyed lying. It was fun. A rush. Tricking people for its own sake, no motive other than the satisfaction of outsmarting the person on the other end of the lie. The compulsive liar. An anarchist's bomb inside the Ministry of Truth.

Matthew Rycroft. He had every reason to lie, and the biggest reason as well. He was facing spending most, if not all of the rest of his life behind bars. He didn't have his lie ready when Chen and Brunelle first confronted him. 'Do you have an alibi? No, not yet'. Not yet indeed, but he got himself a lawyer and then she got him an alibi.

Brunelle paused for a moment as he realized Matt hadn't actually lied to them, not personally anyway. He'd hired a lawyer for that. And put up a friend to do it for him.

James Crossero. Why would he lie? He wasn't in any trouble. To the contrary, lying to the police would get him in trouble he wasn't otherwise facing. Was he trying to get something he didn't think he could get otherwise? What? Or maybe the question was who? Was there more to his friendship with Matt? Is that why he asked Brunelle if he was homophobic? Was he in competition for Matt's affections? If so, he was probably correct that he'd have a better chance with Matt than someone who sold him out to the cops.

Katie Sommers. The one Brunelle was hoping wasn't lying. The one he was counting on to be not lying. The one he decided early on wasn't lying. So, she was probably lying. But about which part? They said the smartest lies were the ones that were mostly true, that only deviated from the truth where needed, and even then no more than absolutely necessary. She was beautiful, and smart. She knew the idea that she wasn't with Matt at all that night was probably too big of a lie. So what part was the lie? How long he was there? When he left? Why he left?

Brunelle frowned at his board. Seattle, Bellevue. Chen, Emory. Rycroft, Sommers, Crossero. He was missing something. He knew it. But he still had a little over a week to figure it out.

It was the other thing he'd forgotten about that was about to explode on him.

CHAPTER 23

Brunelle had stayed late at the office gazing at his crazy board. The next morning, he came in early so he could erase it before anyone else in his office saw it. He took a picture of it first, so he wouldn't lose his work, but he didn't need any of the paralegals or other prosecutors thinking he had finally lost it. There were plenty of young guns who wouldn't mind an office just a few doors down from the big boss and a file cabinet full of murder cases. The last thing he needed was some misstep that made him look like he was losing his edge.

Nicole Richards, the senior paralegal for the homicide unit, stepped into his office just as he erased the last bit of conspiracy babble off the board. One of her hands held some papers. The other was on her hip. She did not look happy.

"You have got to let me do the paralegal stuff, Dave," she scolded. "When you try to be lawyer and paralegal and even detective, this is what happens."

She shoved the papers at him. He hesitated. Her introduction made clear that whatever she was giving him, it wasn't good. And it was his fault.

"*State versus Matthew Rycroft,* Motion to Dismiss," he read aloud. He looked up and grinned. "What else is new?"

Nicole frowned and pointed at the document. "Keep reading."

"Motion to Dismiss," Brunelle returned his gaze to the pleading in his hand, "for Prosecutorial Misconduct." He looked up again. "Ah."

"Yeah, ah," Nicole agreed.

"What did I allegedly do?" He knew she'd already read the entire thing before giving it to him. She wouldn't have been so angry otherwise.

"It's more like what you didn't do," Nicole answered. "Did you interview a witness, then fail to disclose the content of that witness's statement to the defense attorney as required by the criminal court rules and your ethical obligations, not just as an attorney but the heightened ethical mandates placed on you as a prosecutor?"

Brunelle's mouth tightened into a flat line and he nodded as he realized he had dropped a rather large ball. More like a bomb. "James Crossero."

"James Crossero, yes," Nicole repeated even as he was finishing the name himself. "What were you thinking, Dave?"

"I was thinking," Brunelle responded slowly, his mind racing between whether to admit his mistake or defend his actions, all while calculating the peril to his case and maybe even his bar license, "that I wasn't going to just accept what Amanda West told me her alibi witness said. I have a right to interview her witnesses too."

Nicole tipped her head to one side. "Don't bullshit me, Dave. You're not in trouble for interviewing a witness. You're in trouble for not telling the defense attorney what that witness said."

Brunelle rolled his eyes and shook West's motion. "She must know. Otherwise, she wouldn't have known to file this."

"And you know that doesn't matter."

He did know. Discovery in criminal cases was a one-way street. He had to turn over everything to the defense, and they had to turn over practically nothing. Maybe it was more like a five-lane freeway going in one direction and a bike trail going in the other. That was why cops did the interviews. Because they always wrote up a report that summarized what was said, and they always sent the report to the prosecutor's office, and the Nicole Richardses of the prosecutor's office sent a copy of the report to the Amanda Wests of the world because the Dave Brunelles would forget to share what they'd learned since they weren't used to writing up reports. The Dave Brunelles of the world were used to having an audience when they confronted a witness, a courtroom filled with spectators, including those Amanda Wests and their fancy motions to dismiss, so they didn't need to tell anyone.

Brunelle frowned. "Yeah, I know."

All he had to have done was shoot West an email with what little Crossero had added to his original affidavit. He didn't have to send her a written transcript, and if Crossero had said nothing new, then there wouldn't have been anything to send to West. But Crossero did admit he was apart from Rycroft at least a little bit, they did sleep, and they didn't go to the bathroom together. Tiny little cracks in the story. Just barely enough for Brunelle to stick the point of a spear in. Small as the concessions were, they were useful to the prosecution. That was why Brunelle had dragged them out of Crossero. And that was why it was such a big deal he hadn't told West. If he'd waited to bring that out in the middle of cross-examining Crossero at trial, having known it existed without telling the defense, it would have been a violation of Rycroft's right to a prepared, effective attorney.

That's why it mattered.

And that's why he was in deep trouble.

Nicole huffed and shook her head one more time. "Well, let me know if you need anything, Dave. Like maybe I could send out a copy of the summary of the interview you better sit down and write right freaking now."

"Yeah," Brunelle agreed, "I should probably do that."

"I mean, that horse is probably already out of the barn," Nicole said, "but it might make the barn look a little nicer when you're trying to keep the judge from burning it to the ground."

"Nice metaphor," Brunelle managed a half smile. "I might use that in my response."

"Get that done this morning too, Dave," Nicole counseled. "You don't want the judge reading her motion and then having to wait days before hearing your response. They'll have made up their mind by then."

Brunelle nodded again. "You're full of good advice this morning, Nicole."

"Not just this morning," Nicole reminded him. She pointed at his computer. "Now get to work. I'll fetch us both some coffee and we'll do what we can to fix this."

Good ol' Nicole, he thought with a fuller, truer smile. At least someone was on his side.

CHAPTER 24

In truth, there were a lot of people on his side. A whole system of people, in fact. The entire prosecutor's office. Multiple police departments across the county. Forensic agencies like the Medical Examiner's Office and the State Crime Lab. Even the judges, to hear the defense bar tell it. Brunelle knew all that. But it didn't matter if the one person whose support he really wanted was the last one he dared ask it from.

"What's on your mind, Dave?" Emory asked him that night as he lingered over his plate. Hers was already in the sink.

They were having dinner at her place. She had street parking, so he wouldn't have to get up early the next day. That is, if he managed to stay the night with questions like that. Or rather, the answers to questions like that.

"Nothing," Brunelle insisted. They both knew that was a lie, so in a way, it wasn't. "Just work, you know?"

"Mm-hmm, I know," Emory answered. "That Rycroft case?"

Brunelle had other cases, of course, but they didn't have a trial date accelerating at him. Or a motion to dismiss for his misconduct pending, with a hearing set hurriedly just days before that oncoming trial date.

"Yeah," he admitted.

Emory tried to cheer up her boyfriend. "You know, it might be kind of fun to get cross-examined by you. I've never really been on the receiving end of your talents. Well, not your legal talents anyway."

Brunelle couldn't help but respond to that. He flashed a genuine smile, but it lacked staying power. He poked his fork at his plate again.

"What's wrong, Dave?" Emory asked. "It's not like you to let an opening like that pass."

"Pun intended?" he managed to quip.

"There's my Davey!" Emory laughed. "Now, tell Casey what's on your mind, so we can get it off your mind and get on to more enjoyable pursuits."

Brunelle had a choice. Get lucky or get real. Emory's proposition was intended to get the real out of the way first, but he was pretty sure it wouldn't quite work out that way. Still, sometimes the only way out was through.

"I fucked up at work," Brunelle began. "That case."

"Right, your case, my investigation," Emory acknowledged. "What did you fuck up?"

"I interviewed a witness myself," Brunelle explained, "then forgot to tell the defense attorney right away about what the witness said."

"Oops," Emory winced. "That's a big deal, right? I mean between you lawyer types."

Brunelle shrugged. "Intentionally withholding relevant information from a defendant is a big deal. It violates a bunch of their constitutional rights. But accidentally forgetting to tell the defense attorney immediately about some small qualifications to a prior statement that she got herself? I don't think that should be such a big deal. But the defense attorney is trying to make a mountain out of it."

Emory frowned in thought for a moment. "A prior statement she got herself?" she repeated. "Did you interview Crossero? After I already did that for you?"

"You didn't do it for me," Brunelle contradicted. "You did it for Chen."

"After you asked Chen to do it for you," Emory pointed out.

"Whatever," Brunelle pouted. "The point is, I interviewed him but forgot to tell Rycroft's attorney what he said. Now she's trying to make a big deal out of a small mistake, a mistake I've already corrected."

"The point is," Emory replied, "that I already interviewed him once and if you think I did such a terrible job the first time, you should have asked me to do it again. At least I would have written a report."

"You didn't do a bad job," Brunelle insisted, but in a tone that betrayed his true opinion.

"Then why did you need to talk to him again?" Emory crossed her arms and raised an accusing eyebrow higher than Brunelle would have thought possible.

"Because, I don't know," Brunelle stalled before delivering his answer, "I just couldn't leave it alone. If what he said was true, completely true, then my case falls apart."

"Maybe it should then," Emory challenged.

"Or maybe you should have asked him if he and Rycroft ever separated," Brunelle suggested, "because they did."

Emory's eyebrow dropped. "They separated? He didn't

tell me that. What did he tell you?"

"He said they separated a bunch of times," Brunelle answered. "When they went to the bathroom or went to get snacks. They both slept some too and not necessarily at the same time."

Emory stared at him for a moment, then burst out laughing. "That's not separating, you dummy! That's just being over at somebody's house. We're fucking but I don't want you coming to the bathroom with me."

Brunelle didn't like being laughed at. "It matters, Casey. I don't need them to be apart all night. I just need them be apart sometimes. He gave me that."

"He gave you jack shit, Dave," Emory replied, adding his name with the same unfriendly undercurrent his use of hers had carried. "You make a lousy detective."

"Well, I guess that makes two of us," Brunelle grumbled into his plate.

"What," Emory's eyebrows shot up again, "did you just say?"

Brunelle waved his hand at her, but he didn't look up. "Nothing."

"Say it again," she told him. "I want to hear you say it again."

"I didn't mean it, okay?" Brunelle offered a lopsided frown. "I'm sorry. I'm just really frustrated. West could file a bar complaint. I could get suspended for this. I heard about some prosecutor in Maryland who got disbarred for something like this. Everyone agreed it wasn't intentional and they still took his license."

"I know," Emory began as calmly as she could muster, "that I don't work for the big bad Seattle Police Department. I know I work for a suburban agency. I know Bellevue is rich and safe and we don't have nearly as many murders as Seattle. Hell, we have maybe one a year, and I know I'm not the detective who gets to handle that."

Brunelle frowned but couldn't muster himself to look up from his plate.

"Do you know how hard it is to do this job as a woman? As a Black woman? Of course, you don't. But I do. They can chalk it up to seniority, but there's a reason Black women like me don't have seniority. So, I have to just smile and accept it because I haven't been there for thirty years like the good old boys ahead of me."

"Casey," Brunelle tried again, "I said I'm sorry."

"But I am a very good detective, David Brunelle," Emory continued. "I work hard on my cases, and I solve my cases. I care about the people I help and, hell, I even care about the people I arrest. And I cared enough about you to help you and your work husband, the Great Detective Larry Chen, when I easily could have handed it off to one of those good old boys ready to retire as soon as they max out their pensions. But I didn't do that. I did you a favor and I did a hell of a job.

"You think because you asked some questions that might fool a jury in the heat of a trial that you have more insight than me? That you could be a better detective than me? Ha! There's a reason I didn't ask those questions, Dave. It's because they're stupid. I don't need to ask if Rycroft went to the bathroom alone. I need to know if he left the house alone, which he didn't, and which I verified with his phone records. And do you know why I don't care if he went to the bathroom alone, Dave? Because Charlie Rycroft wasn't murdered in a fucking bathroom in Bellevue. He was murdered in his own apartment, twenty minutes away in Seattle."

"That's what you think," Brunelle went ahead and engaged the argument after all. It didn't seem like she was going to accept his apology. "And I think you're wrong."

Emory grinned and shook her head at him. "That defense attorney isn't afraid of what you so amazingly uncovered," she laughed. "She just knows you fucked up and she's going to make you pay for it. I guess," she looked him dead in the eye, "that means you aren't a very good prosecutor."

Brunelle dropped his fork with a clang. He leaned back in his chair and placed a hand over his mouth, exhaling through his fingers. Finally, he pulled his hand away and said, "I think maybe I better leave. Before one of us says something we can't take back."

Emory looked away. "I think that's a good idea," she agreed. Then, "I hope it's not too late."

Brunelle pushed out his chair and stood up. "I hope so too."

CHAPTER 25

"Don't look at me for sympathy," Chen said before he took a bite of his burger. "I think she has a point."

Brunelle had invited Chen out to lunch, his treat or Chen might not have come. Ostensibly, it was to check in before the trial started in a week. Make sure they were on the same page and all those other metaphors. But mostly it was for Brunelle to find out what Chen thought about his argument with Emory.

"You think I shouldn't have interviewed Crossero?" Brunelle asked. "Why didn't you stop me when I called you for his ID photo?"

"I didn't say that," Chen manages to say as he finished his bite. "I said she has a point. You doing that undercut her investigation. You probably should have had her do it. You wouldn't be in the trouble you're in if you had."

"I'm not in that much trouble," Brunelle claimed. "Not yet anyway."

"Did that defense attorney file a bar complaint yet?"

Brunelle frowned. "No. That's the not yet part."

"Probably waiting until after the hearing," Chen surmised. "It will be a lot more serious if a judge makes a formal finding that you violated your ethics, and Rycroft's rights."

Brunelle knew that was true. It just made the stakes even higher for his hearing on the motion to dismiss.

"It was an honest mistake," Brunelle insisted.

"So was telling Casey she wasn't a very good detective," Chen observed. "That doesn't mean there won't be consequences. How many people did you put in prison for honest mistakes that also happened to be crimes?"

Brunelle thought for a moment. "Probably too many."

"Probably," Chen agreed. "So, what are you going to do?"

Brunelle thought for a moment and agreed. "I suppose I'll admit I should have provided West the information sooner, but point out that she has it now, in plenty of time to be prepared for trial, so there's no prejudice and the motion should be denied."

Chen stared at Brunelle as he sipped the last of his drink through his straw, loudly. "No, dummy. What are you going to do about Casey?"

"Oh, uh, I'm not sure," Brunelle admitted. "I'm not always very good at relationships when the going starts getting rough."

"You're never good at relationships when the going gets rough," Chen answered.

Brunelle supposed that might be true.

"You want some advice?" Chen asked.

"That's why I bought you lunch," Brunelle said it out loud.

"Just don't do anything stupid," Chen said.

Brunelle offered a nervous smile. "Who, me?"

CHAPTER 26

The hearing on West's *second* motion to dismiss was scheduled again for 9:00 a.m. in the morning, and again in front of Judge Jonathan Richter. There was little chance anymore that they would get any other judge for the trial, and it made even less sense for them to get a different judge for this particular motion. To Brunelle's chagrin. It had been Richter whom Brunelle had promised he would not be calling James Crossero in his case-in-chief. Now he would have to explain why he went out and interviewed Crossero anyway right after that winning promise. And, according to West anyway, tried to keep it secret.

Often, perhaps even usually, Brunelle enjoyed arriving for an argument, although that may have been, he could admit, because he often, perhaps even usually, won the hearing. One of the perks of being the prosecutor. That morning, however, he entered Judge Richter's courtroom with more than a little trepidation. This wasn't an argument about what the defendant had done wrong or what the cops had done wrong or maybe even what the crime lab had done wrong. No. He, the prosecutor, was the one being accused of wrongdoing, and he did not like it one bit.

He was aware of the irony.

"Good morning, Mr. Brunelle," West greeted him in a sing-song voice as he reached the lawyers' tables at the front of the courtroom. Her client was already seated at the defense table, a guard hovering within lunging distance in case he did anything stupid. "Lovely day for a dismissal, isn't it? Perhaps you'd like to offer my client a misdemeanor and credit for time served before the judge comes out?"

"Why would he accept that?" Brunelle grumbled. "I thought he was innocent."

"Well, never mind then," West chucked. "We're not here to talk about him anyway. Are we?"

Brunelle offered something between a sneer and a grimace. A sneer because he was irritated at her; a grimace because she was right. The only thing worse than the coal-raking he was about to endure from Richter was making small talk with West while they waited for the judge to take the bench. That was why Brunelle had gone ahead and been four minutes later than usual; so that after one more minute, the bailiff would stand up and call out.

"All rise! The King County Superior Court is in session, The Honorable Jonathan Richter presiding."

"You may be seated," Richter instructed as he took his own seat, albeit several feet above everyone else. "Are the parties ready to proceed on the matter of *The State of Washington versus Matthew Rycroft*? Proceed *again*, I suppose I could say."

Brunelle had remained standing to address the Court. "The State is ready, Your Honor."

"The defense is ready as well, Your Honor," West answered. Brunelle wondered if she'd do that thing where she stood the whole time again.

Richter smiled down at the lawyers and shook his head slightly. "Well, I can assure you, I have read all of the briefing on this motion. I'm curious to see where the oral arguments go." He looked at the prosecution table. "As much as I'm looking forward especially to hearing from you, Mr. Brunelle, this is the defendant's motion, so I will hear first from Ms. West."

"Thank you, Your Honor," she acknowledged and took a deep breath.

Brunelle went ahead and sat down. He knew it could take a while, and he knew he'd rather be sitting down while it did.

"This motion is brought under Criminal Court Rule 8.3(b), which states, and I quote, 'The court, in the furtherance of justice, after notice and hearing, may dismiss any criminal prosecution due to arbitrary action or governmental misconduct when there has been prejudice to the rights of the accused which materially affect the accused's right to a fair trial'. It is also brought under the Fifth Amendment of the United States Constitution, which states, in pertinent part, 'In all criminal prosecutions, the accused shall enjoy the right to be confronted with the witnesses against him, and to have the Assistance of Counsel for his defence'. It is also brought under Article One, Section Twenty-Two of the Washington State Constitution, which states, again, in pertinent part, 'In criminal prosecutions the accused shall have the right to appear and defend in person, or by counsel, to demand the nature and cause of the accusation against him, to have a copy thereof, and to meet the witnesses against him face to face'."

Brunelle was glad he sat down.

"Further, Your Honor, the Washington State Bar Rule of Professional Conduct 3.8, titled 'Special Responsibilities of a

Prosecutor', states at subsection (d), 'The prosecutor in a criminal case shall make timely disclosure to the defense of all evidence or information known to the prosecutor that tends to negate the guilt of the accused or mitigates the offense'."

"Thank you, Ms. West," Judge Richter finally interjected. "As I mentioned, I have read the briefing. I think I'm familiar with both the legal and ethical standards at issue here. Perhaps you could jump ahead to how you believe Mr. Brunelle's conduct violated those standards?"

"Yes, Your Honor," West responded. "As I'm sure the Court recalls, Mr. Brunelle stood before Your Honor not a month ago and assured this Court that he had no interest in calling James Crossero to the stand at trial, despite the fact that Mr. Crossero is the one witness who sheds the most light on what actually happened in this case, and on the incontrovertible fact that my client is absolutely, one hundred percent innocent."

I can controvert it, Brunelle thought, his chin on his fist.

"Indeed," West continued, "Your Honor made special note of Mr. Brunelle's assurances that he had no interest in Mr. Crossero's testimony when ruling in favor of the State and denying my earlier motion to dismiss. And so, Your Honor, you can only imagine my utter shock and confusion when I learned that Mr. Brunelle left Your Honor's courtroom and practically drove directly to Mr. Crossero's place of employment to confront him about his knowledge of the case, badgering him in an effort to make him change his story. And Your Honor can imagine how much greater that shock and confusion were when I had to learn that from a third party rather than from Mr. Brunelle himself, despite his very clear, very mandatory obligations to disclose such information, as enumerated in the court rules and constitutions of The State of Washington and

The United States of America."

Brunelle glanced around for a flag or two for West to wave. But they were behind the judge, of course.

"I can imagine," Judge Richter said, but more in a tone to encourage her to get on with it than one of commiseration.

"I won't go into who I learned it from that Mr. Brunelle had obtained additional information from a key witness in this case," West said, "except to say that it was not, as it should have been, Mr. Brunelle himself. Had I not learned of this through my own means, then this motion would not have been noted and we would have conducted this trial with Mr. Brunelle possessing relevant information about the case which was completely unknown to the defense. I would have asked questions of prospective jurors, delivered my opening statement, cross-examined the State's witnesses, and conducted the direct-examination of Mr. Crossero, all without knowing the surprise Mr. Brunelle intended to spring on all of us, Your Honor included, when, finally, in the middle of the defense's case-in-chief, he stood up to cross-examine Mr. Crossero, having already done so in secret on the sidewalk outside of P.N.W. Outfitters weeks earlier."

That did sound pretty nefarious, Brunelle had to admit.

"But for my discovering this deception," West continued, "but for my filing this motion to flush out this subterfuge, but for my pulling this dark stain on the prosecutor profession into the purifying light of day, we would never have known what Mr. Brunelle had done. Your Honor would never have known. Certainly not until it was too late, and maybe not ever. Perhaps Mr. Brunelle would have succeeded in tricking all of us. Perhaps we all would have been agog at his amazingly incisive cross-examination of the defense's key witness that we would have just chalked it up to some good old-fashioned lawyering. Because surely it couldn't have been more than that. Certainly Mr. Brunelle wouldn't have done something unethical. Certainly Mr. Brunelle wouldn't have cheated."

West threw a sharp glance at Brunelle. He didn't turn fully to see it, but he could feel it.

"But he did cheat, Your Honor. He tried to, anyway. But he got caught with his hand in the cookie jar. And the only just and fair and right thing for this honorable Court to do is dismiss this case for the egregious, unforgivable, irremediable conduct of Mr. Brunelle. Thank you."

Damn, Brunelle thought. He almost wished he were that conniving and evil. He probably wouldn't have been caught.

"Thank you, Ms. West," Judge Richter said, "for that... passionate advocacy. I will hear now from the State. Mr. Brunelle?"

Brunelle pushed himself out of his chair. He tugged at his suit coat and buttoned it, since he expected to be on his feet for more than a few moments. He took a deep breath. Then he began.

"I'm sorry," he said. "I apologize. I apologize to Ms. West. I apologize to Mr. Rycroft. And I apologize to the Court."

Contrition was disarming. At least that was what Brunelle had found over the years of being paid twice a month to battle against opponent after opponent after opponent. It took courage to fight when you were right. It took even more to admit when you were wrong. And it usually won the battle after all.

While it was admission of a transgression, an apology was very much not an agreement that the admitted transgression warranted the punishment sought.

"I made a mistake, and I will own that," he continued, "but Ms. West is incorrect that my mistake requires dismissal of the charges. To the contrary, the standard set by the court rules, the case law, and yes, even the constitution, is very much against dismissal."

He was going to thread the needle. It was going to rely on technicalities and sound very loop-holey. He knew he better acknowledge that too.

"The argument I'm about to make will be rule-based, Your Honor. It will sound like I am trying to weasel my way out of my mistake. But I assure you, that is not what I am doing. As I make my argument, please keep in mind that I started my remarks with an apology. Then, at the end of my argument, I will ask you to deny the defendant's motion to dismiss, notwithstanding my apology."

Richter seemed intrigued. He leaned forward and gestured for Brunelle to continue. *Good.*

West seemed worried. She shifted uneasily in her seat and glued her eyes onto Brunelle. *Even better.*

"To begin with, Your Honor," Brunelle started the legal analysis portion of his presentation, "the law does not require the prosecutor to turn over all information in our possession. We routinely do that anyway, because it's easier and it's safer and it keeps our options open. The court rules, including Rule of Professional Conduct 3.8, only require that a prosecutor turn over information we intend to use at trial. However, I have already assured this Court that I would not be calling Mr. Crossero as a witness in my case-in-chief. Therefore, anything he might have said could not have been, by definition, anything I would have intended to use at trial."

Definitely technicality/loop-holey. But also accurate.

"A prosecutor is also obligated to turn over information which tends to negate or even cast doubt on a defendant's guilt regardless of whether we intend to use it," Brunelle proceeded, "but again, Your Honor, there was nothing in what I learned from Mr. Crossero that was in any way helpful to the defendant. To the contrary, it supported the idea that the defendant might have had, even according to Mr. Crossero's version of events, sufficient time to slip away and commit the murder. That information was in no way exculpatory, and therefore I was in no way obligated to turn it over to the defense."

He paused for a moment to take the temperature of the courtroom. It was one thing to defend yourself. It was another to be defiant. Defiance invited an assertion of dominance. Not something Brunelle was looking for from the judge just then.

"Allow me to clarify, Your Honor," he took a breath, "that I know it would have been better to pass on what I learned to Ms. West immediately. Just because I wasn't under an absolute obligation to do so doesn't mean it wouldn't have been the right thing to do. I remember as a young prosecutor being mentored once by an older prosecutor when we were discussing whether we should turn over some piece of evidence. 'If we're talking about it,' she said, 'then we turn it over.' That, of course, is the more prudent, and more just course of action. But it doesn't mean it's the legally required one."

He wasn't sure if he'd managed sufficient contrition in that particular portion of his argument, but he didn't want to beat a dead apology, so he moved on.

"I think the most important thing to keep in mind, Your Honor, is that, while Criminal Rule 8.3(b) does allow a court to dismiss a criminal case for governmental misconduct, or even just mismanagement, it only authorizes such an extreme remedy if there has actually been prejudice to the defendant. So, I ask, what prejudice is there? The information has been turned over. Trial is still a week away. And the State will still not be calling James Crossero as a witness. Should I have passed on the information immediately? Yes. Did I do so once reminded by the defendant's motion? Also yes. Is the defense now in possession of that information sufficiently in advance of trial to be able to use it in whatever way they see fit to prepare for that trial? Absolutely yes."

Time to bring it home.

"In summary, then, Your Honor. I wasn't obligated to turn the information over at all, but I wish I had. I should have done it sooner, but I did it soon enough. This is an embarrassment to me and how I wish to perform my job, but it is not a basis to dismiss this case. I made a mistake, Your Honor. I implore you not to make one as well. Please deny the defendant's motion to dismiss. Thank you."

Richter leaned back in his chair and rubbed a hand over his mouth as he nodded thoughtfully.

"May I respond?" West asked. She stood up hastily to ask the question and her voice betrayed her agitation.

"Of course," Judge Richter allowed. "It's your motion. What would you like to say?"

"I would like to say, Your Honor, that the prosecutor is hardly the one who should get to say whether his misconduct has prejudiced the defendant. Yes, trial is still a week away, but I was not about to begin my preparation only seven days before the beginning of a first-degree murder trial. The extent to which his failure to timely disclose this information has prejudiced the defense is not for him to know. It is for me and my client to know, and I am averring to the court that we have indeed been prejudiced."

'Averring'? Brunelle thought. Only a civil lawyer would use that word. Brunelle wasn't even sure he knew what it actually meant.

"Thank you, Ms. West," Judge Richter accepted the additional argument like an ocean accepting another drop of rain. "I believe I am ready to make my ruling."

Brunelle's heart sped up. No prosecutor wanted their case dismissed out from under them. But this was a first-degree murder case, and the reason for the dismissal—God forbid—would be his personal mistake. One that the bar association might take issue with next if a judicial officer found it sufficiently egregious to dismiss that aforementioned first-degree murder case. It wasn't just the case that was on the line. It was his career.

"Mr. Brunelle was correct to apologize," Richter began. "He made a mistake. He never should have interviewed a witness by himself anyway. In addition to leading to just this sort of motion, it's simply poor trial practice. What if Mr. Crossero had admitted the alibi he provided the defendant was a complete fabrication, but then testified at trial that it was the truth? Who would Mr. Brunelle call as a witness as to his statement to you that it was a lie? No one. Because he brought no witness with him. So, bad on you, Mr. Brunelle, in more ways than one. But also, apology accepted. I appreciate you acknowledging your mistake, rather than trying to spin it as anything other than that."

Brunelle gave a nod of thanks up to the judge, but he knew not to interrupt with actual words.

"It being established that Mr. Brunelle failed to provide the information in a timely manner, I look next to Mr. Brunelle's claim that he was actually under no obligation to turn it over because it was not helpful to the defendant and he did not intend to use it in his case-in-chief in any event. I am, to put it mildly, less impressed by this argument. I do not believe it can be for the prosecutor to decide what information is to be turned over to the defense. There is no way for the prosecution to truly know how some additional piece of information might impact the ability of a lawyer to defend a client. On the whole, I have found defense attorneys to be often more creative than their counterparts in the prosecutor's office. It may be because their job requires more creativity to help their clients to get out of the trouble they find themselves in. But in any case, you don't get to decide what is turned over to the defense. Your mentor was correct, Mr. Brunelle. If you thought the information was important enough to gather, then it was also important enough to disclose."

Damn, Brunelle thought. He was 1-1 on his arguments. Time for the tie-breaker. He crossed his fingers.

"Which brings me to Mr. Brunelle's final point," Judge Richter said. "Prejudice. I agree with Ms. West that, again, the prosecutor cannot be the one who gets to determine whether the defendant has been prejudiced, any more than they should be permitted to decide whether to disclose information in the first place. But,"

Brunelle was really hoping he was going to like what was on the other side of that 'but'.

"I don't believe the defense attorney can be the sole arbiter of that determination either. If it were left to sole discretion of the defense attorney, then every violation would be prejudicial, and that portion of the rule would be rendered effectively meaningless."

Brunelle liked that well enough.

"No, I think the proper approach," Richter continued, "and the one contemplated by the rule itself, is that the defense alleges prejudice, the prosecution denies it, and then the court decides whether the defendant was indeed prejudiced and, if so, whether the prejudice rises to the level where dismissal is the appropriate remedy."

Brunelle nodded slightly. He just hoped Richter agreed with him that there wasn't prejudice. At least not enough to dump a Murder One case.

"I do think there was some prejudice, of course," Richter said. "The delay between when Mr. Brunelle should have produced the information and when he actually did so is that much less time the defense had to prepare for it. I'm going to call that procedural prejudice. There's a reason we have the rules we have, and violating them gives rise, perhaps even automatically, to this procedural form of prejudice. So, I am finding that."

Damn, thought Brunelle.

"However," Richter continued

Un-damn. Maybe.

"I think there needs to be more than procedural prejudice," Richter said. "I think there needs to be some sort of substantive prejudice. The information that was withheld, would it have been beneficial to the defense? Would it likely have come out some other way eventually? And if so, would it have been better or worse for the defense to come out at the later time?"

Brunelle wasn't sure where Richter was headed. But Richter clearly understood what he meant to say.

"First," he ticked off a finger, "the information Mr.

Brunelle obtained could hardly be deemed helpful to the defense. Mr. Brunelle essentially cross-examined Mr. Crossero on that city sidewalk and got him to admit that it was at least not impossible that the defendant might have possibly, maybe slipped out unnoticed to commit the crime he is accused of. That, it seems to me, is not helpful to the defense, and therefore failure to turn it over in a timely manner was less prejudicial than something obviously favorable to the defendant.

"Second," another finger ticked off, "I do think that information was likely to be elicited at some point before the end of the case, most likely during Mr. Brunelle's cross-examination, should the defense have called Mr. Crossero as a witness, which they have indicated they would. Mr. Brunelle essentially previewed his cross-examination in advance of the trial, which leads me to the third point."

The judge ticked a final finger. "I cannot say that it is prejudicial for the defense to have received this information in advance of the actual cross-examination of Mr. Crossero at trial. To the contrary, it is probably beneficial to them. Rather than have this sort of potentially incriminating evidence appear for the first time during live testimony, with no opportunity to respond other than try to rehabilitate the witness with some hastily conceived redirect examination, Ms. West has been afforded an opportunity to look into these alleged deficiencies in her client's alibi and shore them up in advance of the trial, before opening statements even."

Richter shook his head. "No, I cannot say there has been prejudice to the defendant. Quite the contrary, in my estimation. And therefore, the standard enumerated in Criminal Rule 8.3(b) governing dismissal of a criminal case for prosecutorial misconduct has not been met. Accordingly, the defendant's motion to dismiss is denied."

He raised an eyebrow down at Brunelle and added, "Notwithstanding the prosecutor's admitted mistake."

Brunelle had never been so relieved to be ineffective. He had screwed up, but he couldn't even do that in a way that helped his case. It had helped West. And so he had dodged a bullet.

The hearing was over, and Richter excused himself from the bench. The guard moved in and took control of Rycroft to return him to his cell. The bailiff and the court reporter disappeared to their offices behind, and West stepped over to Brunelle's table.

"You were smart to start with an apology," she said. "The judge accepted it."

Brunelle nodded in agreement but any joy he felt from winning the hearing ebbed away.

Richter had accepted his apology.

Why didn't Casey?

CHAPTER 27

Part of the fun of winning in court was leaving court and telling people that you won. A big part. The best part, at least sometimes, maybe after that whole 'justice' thing. But after winning—*i.e.*, barely escaping—his second motion to dismiss on the *State versus Rycroft* case, Brunelle's options for celebration were limited. He didn't have co-counsel on this one, a fact he was becoming increasingly relieved about. Nicole wasn't at her desk. Chen didn't answer. And he wasn't about to call Emory. Not on that motion. Not on those facts. Not about that witness.

As a result, Brunelle was more susceptible than he might otherwise have been when his phone rang, and the lovely Katie Sommers's breathy voice floated over the line to fill his ear, and mind.

"Mr. Brunelle, sir? This is Katherine Sommers. I really need to see you."

She really was lovely. And almost half his age. And a witness in his murder case. And something else he was having trouble remembering right then.

"Uh, Ms. Sommers," he stammered. "It's, uh, good to

hear from you. What is it that you want to talk about?"

Then he remembered the something else.

"And shouldn't Mr. Nicholson be the one calling me? He still represents you, right?"

No, that wasn't it after all.

"It's complicated," Sommers said for at least the second time when talking with Brunelle. "Can you come see me? I heard you've been talking to some of the witnesses yourself, and I have information about the case. But I really want to tell you face-to-face. Alone."

Fortunately, the answer was simple. He couldn't talk to her without Nicholson. And he'd almost lost the entire case for doing exactly that sort of in-person interview of a key witness without a detective accompanying him. Plus, that other something crouching in the back of his mind. Easy decision.

"I can be at your apartment in thirty minutes."

She really was very lovely.

CHAPTER 28

The Roosevelt neighborhood was only about five miles north of downtown, straight up Interstate-5. There was a combined freeway exit for Roosevelt and Green Lake, a small inland lake with a city park wrapped around it and one hell of a fish-and-chips restaurant across from the main park entrance. At the bottom of the off-ramp, turn left for Green Lake. Turn right for huge mistakes.

He turned right and followed Ravenna Boulevard to Roosevelt Avenue, but it was one-way southbound, so he had to go straight to 12th Avenue, turned left, then left again on 50th Street, and finally another left back onto Roosevelt. There was one parking spot available, directly across from the photography studio and the somehow-still-in-business records and CD store. It was one-hour parking. He didn't suppose he'd last that long anyway.

The interview, he corrected in his head. *The interview won't last that long anyway.*

He shook his head, parked the car, and stepped out onto the sidewalk. It was a nice enough day. Warm, but not too warm. Like most of Seattle, both the weather and the people.

The entrance to Katie Sommers's apartment complex was just up from where he'd parked. He traversed the distance before he had time to think about why he shouldn't be doing so. He recalled her apartment number from his previous visit with Chen. Again, with far too insufficient of hesitation, he pressed the button next to the label reading '205'.

After the briefest of waits, Sommers's voice came over the intercom. "David? I mean, Mr. Brunelle?"

It had been a long time since a woman had called him 'David'. Too long. Or maybe not long enough.

"Ms. Sommers?" he responded. "Yes, this is Dave Brunelle. Can you buzz me in? That is, if you'd still like to talk?"

"Talk?" Sommers seemed to giggle. "Yes, of course. Talk." The door buzzed. "Come inside, David. Please."

Brunelle pulled the door open and stepped inside. It seemed dimmer than he remembered, and there was a strong smell he hadn't noticed before either. It wasn't bad, just apparent. Laundry detergent maybe, or incense. Whatever it was, it was pleasant enough. He decided to take the elevator so he wouldn't be winded when he reached her door. Not that one flight of stairs would necessarily make him winded, but he didn't want to take the chance.

205. There was a different smell at her door. Fresher. Sweeter. Better. He took a moment to linger in it, then knocked.

The door swung open immediately. Katie Sommers hung in the doorway, her blonde hair cascading over bare shoulders, her sleeveless silk blouse pulling to escape from her red pencil skirt. And heels. Really tall heels.

"Thank you for coming, David." She blinked slowly, showing off expert makeup and long lashes. "I mean, Mr.

Brunelle. Thank you for coming, Mr. Brunelle."

She stepped back and beckoned Brunelle into her apartment. He didn't hesitate. The sweet smell was stronger inside. Flowers, he was pretty sure. The shades were half drawn, covered in thin red fabric. Candles burned on the coffee table, adding their acrid aroma pleasantly to the floral smell Brunelle was able to confirm was her perfume when she sat down right next to him on her leather couch.

"I need to tell you something, Mr. Brunelle, sir," she breathed. Her breath was somehow even sweeter than her perfume. "Something about the case."

Brunelle nodded, almost hypnotized. Then his brain recognized the phrase 'the case'. It shook him from his reverie. "The case," he repeated. He scooted an inch or two away from her. "Right. Yes, the case. You wanted to talk about the case."

"Yes, you se—" she began, but Brunelle interrupted her.

"Wait." He pulled his phone out of his pocket, a rather awkward movement on that leather couch. "I agreed to come because, um, I figured we could make it work by calling your lawyer and having him on the line."

"You want my lawyer to listen in?" Sommers snarled a lip at the suggestion.

"Well, I mean, not to—" Brunelle began, but he stopped himself. "It's just that, um, he is your lawyer, and so, technically, I'm not supposed to talk to you without him present, and—"

She slid a bit toward him, closing the gap he had opened up. "I don't want him between us."

"I can see that, yes," Brunelle acknowledged, "but it's not really up to you. The RPCs—that is, the Rules of Professional Conduct, the ethical rules that lawyers have to follow—those are kind of lawyer-to-lawyer. If I talk to you without Nick knowing, then it's his right to complain, not yours. Because, you see, I'm breaking a rule designed to protect him, not you."

Sommers grinned and blinked her lidded eyes slowly. "I don't need protection, David. I'm a big girl."

She was, he had certainly noticed, and in all the right places.

"Um, yes," he agreed. Then he swiped open his phone and dialed Nicholson's number anyway.

Sommers leaned back against the couch with a sigh as Nicholson's receptionist answered.

"Good afternoon. Law Offices of Nicholas Nicholson. Are you a prospective new client?"

"Yes, I am," Brunelle answered.

He covered the phone with his hand and whispered to Sommers, "It's the only way to get him on the phone."

Then he spoke to the receptionist again. "It's a felony assault. I'm looking at a lot of time. I own my home and I have a retirement account I could liquidate."

"One moment, please," the receptionist said hurriedly. "I will put you through to Mr. Nicholson."

A few moments later, Nick Nicholson's terrible voice cut through Katie Sommers's wonderful apartment. "Nick Nicholson. How can I help you?"

"Nick. It's Dave," Brunelle said. "I'm here with—"

"Dave, God damn it!" Nicholson shouted. "You have got to stop lying to my receptionist. You're going to get her in trouble."

"With who?" Brunelle asked.

"With me," Nicholson laughed. "She should recognize your voice by now. What did you tell her this time?"

"I told her I owned my home and had a fat retirement account," Brunelle explained.

"Oh, well, okay." Nicholson sounded placated. "Then she was right to put you through. What do you want, Dave? I haven't talked to Katie in weeks. I don't even know if she's still around."

Brunelle looked at the beautiful woman perched to his left. "Oh, she's still around, Nick. In fact, that's why I'm calling. She reached out to me—"

"Oh, great," Nicholson interjected, without a trace of sarcasm. "Good. I don't know why I always have to be involved in everything. She hired me because she was afraid you were gonna charge her with a crime or something. I don't know. She probably did something, right? She's smart enough not to tell you, but she didn't tell me either."

"Yeah, Nick, so here's the thing—" Brunelle tried again.

"But look, I'm glad she's contacting you directly now," Nicholson interrupted again. "Honestly, she's already earned out her retainer. I didn't charge her enough to sit in on three interviews, and we haven't even talked about ponying up more money if she wants me to hold her hand when she testifies."

Brunelle looked over at Sommers. 'More money'? she mouthed with perfect red lips, then shook her head definitively. It sent her hair bouncing.

"I mean, as far as I'm concerned," Nicholson continued, "I've done what I was paid for. She's on her own now unless she wants to pay me more. So, go ahead, talk to her. Be my guest. Just stop calling me and taking up valuable new client time. I have a business to run. Knock yourself out, Dave. She's all yours."

Before Brunelle could protest, Nicholson was gone. And

Brunelle was alone with the lovely Katie Sommers in her Xanadu-like apartment.

She parted those perfect red lips and smiled at him. "I'm all yours, huh?"

Brunelle knew what came next. He should. He'd done it before. Still stinging from the argument with a girlfriend of a long enough duration that it was time to make decisions about moving forward or moving on. Handed an opportunity to allow that decision to be made for him, albeit still by him in its own way. Aware that the shiny new thing preening in front of him was fleeting at best, but not quite illusory. It would destroy so much, including his case and maybe even his career, but he'd rebuilt before. He could be strong in his intentions, but he would always be weak in his desires. And she did smell so damn good.

"It seems that way," Brunelle gazed around the perfectly staged apartment. The door to the bedroom was open; he could see the bed, made up with billowing sheets and turned down for his arrival. He stood up.

"So," he shoved his hands in his pockets, "what did you want to tell me?"

Sommers looked confused for a moment. "Um, you want to talk about that now?"

"Well, yeah." Brunelle shrugged. "I didn't have to fuck Crossero before he agreed to talk to me."

Sommers's mouth fell open. "Wha—What?"

"I. Didn't. Have. To. Fuck. Crossero." Brunelle enunciated each word. "Did you not hear me?"

"I, I heard you," Sommers stammered. "I just didn't, I mean, I don't, I mean, are you sure?"

"Am I sure I didn't fuck James Crossero?" Brunelle

asked. "Yeah, I'm pretty sure. It was outside, in the middle of South Lake Union District. I feel like I would have remembered that."

Sommers's expression finally hardened. So did her posture, from pliant and inviting, to rigid and angry. "Were you just playing me?"

"I kind of feel like it's the other way around," Brunelle responded. "I noticed the first thing you said to me was that you knew I was talking to other witnesses. The only other witness I talked to was Crossero. He's also the one who is saying the exact opposite of what you told us. I figured maybe you were worried I'd start to believe him over you, so maybe you could give me a reason to stay on Team Katie."

He gestured around the bordello-like apartment, finishing at her silk-wrapped figure. "Don't think I wasn't tempted. I was. I am. It would hurt someone I'm mad at, and more importantly, it would hurt me. I mean, not at first. Just the opposite, right? That's kind of the whole point. But I'm getting older now. I don't want to hurt people. And I guess I don't want to hurt myself anymore either."

He reached into his jacket pocket and pulled out one of Chen's cards. "Here. I don't really think you have anything to add to your statement, but if you do, he's your man. Not me. Not now. Not ever."

Brunelle turned and headed for the exit.

"Your loss," she called out after him.

He knew that. Boy, did he know. But there could be bigger losses, and he knew that too.

CHAPTER 29

Brunelle got into his car and headed back toward the freeway. The southbound on-ramp was sort of hidden, as were a lot of the freeway entrances in Seattle. He always figured it was the native Seattleites' latent but simmering dislike of out-of-towners that led the local engineers to have no signage other than a small green sign with only the words 'Freeway Entrance' on it at most on-ramps. No number of the freeway, no direction of travel, certainly no destination cities to help orient the confused interloper. He was surprised they had never built an entrance to Interstate-5 where the on-ramp split into two lanes, each marked 'Vancouver'—one north to the better-known metropolis in Canada and the other to the lesser-known American city of the same name just north of Portland, but with no way to know which was which unless you'd grown up there, and if you hadn't you should go back home anyway.

To get to the on-ramp from Sommers's apartment required a right turn back onto Ravenna Blvd., a U-turn at the next traffic light, and advanced knowledge that what appeared to just be a gap between the giant cement pylons holding up the overpasses was in fact the entrance that would, for some terribly designed reason, spill you onto the far-left side of the southbound lanes of Interstate-5.

All of that alone would have made it difficult to navigate home at any given time, but right then, Brunelle was still distracted by his encounter with Katie the Siren. Before he knew it, he had driven well past that U-turn and the freeway and found himself at the three-way stop where Ravenna Blvd. dead-ended into Green Lake Way, the lake glistening invitingly ahead of him through his windshield.

He could have turned left and snaked his way back to the freeway through the side streets, but instead he turned right and headed for the entrance to the park. It was a nice day for a walk. And he needed to blow off some of that steam that had built up inside him at Chez Sommers, despite his better angels.

He parked his car and stepped out into the day. The sun shone on his face, and he took a deep breath of the relatively fresh air around the lake. Then again, it smelled like a small lake, so that wasn't necessarily great. He wasn't a fisherman; that much had been established. But he enjoyed a walk in the sun as much as anyone, especially when he needed to clear his head — and other body parts.

There was a paved walking/biking path that went all the way around the lake. The complete circuit was almost 3 miles, and Brunelle was wearing a suit. But a leisurely pace would allow him the stamina to complete the loop and also the time to go over things in his head.

He was going to have to tell West about his encounter with Sommers. Not that Sommers actually said anything about the case, but he didn't need to be in front of Richter a third time trying to avoid a dismissal for his allegedly improper actions, especially when he'd stopped himself from acting improperly. For the most part anyway. He probably could have stopped at the door to her apartment. Or on the phone. But he was going to take the moral win and not beat himself up for how late he got it.

The bigger problem was what Sommer's attempted gambit suggested about the case. She was worried Brunelle would believe Crossero over her. And she didn't think her words alone were going to be enough to convince him. That would seem to undercut the reliability of those words. Crossero hadn't even offered to sleep with him, so he must have been confident in his story. Or Brunelle wasn't his type. Although, if Brunelle was honest with himself, he knew he wasn't actually Katie Sommers's type either.

"On your left!" a bicyclist called out, unnecessarily Brunelle thought, since the paint on the asphalt made clear that the bike lane was to the left of the walking lane.

Brunelle slowed for a moment to watch the cyclist speed past him. Generally, the pace around the lake was slow, but there was always someone who thought everything was a race.

Brunelle knew the cliché about life being a marathon instead of a sprint, but he'd come to see it as a relay, handing off to yourself. And not one of those 4 x 400m track relays where every leg is the same, or even that individual medley swimmers do where they swim the length of the pool four different ways. No, every leg was a different length, requiring a different style of running, with no advance warning of what it would be until you had the baton in your hand. And there were the times when you botched the hand-off, when the baton fell to the ground and you had to crouch down on all fours, fumbling for the stupid metal cylinder even as all the other runners flew past you like a cyclist on the left. And when you finally wrapped your fingers around the baton and stood up again, no matter how far behind you were, the only option you had was to start running again.

On the far side of the lake, the path bent around an old shack where people could rent kayaks. Again, Brunelle was in a suit, and again, he wasn't really an outdoorsman. He could admire the people venturing out on to the lake, but he wasn't going to join them. There was probably some metaphor about kayaks and life, but it wasn't coming to him just then, and he realized he was just using musings on the nature of existence to avoid thinking about the case.

And he realized he was using thinking about the case to avoid thinking about Casey.

Maybe because there were too many thoughts. A hundred relay batons bouncing off the rubberized track.

He pulled his jacket tight against the sudden chill of the afternoon breeze and quickened his gait. He couldn't use the case anymore to avoid thinking about Casey, because he'd realized he was doing it. So, he tried to clear his mind of everything and focus on his footfalls on the path and the parking lot ahead of him.

That didn't work either.

Why was he so angry at her? Why was she so angry at him? He was just doing his job. Like she was doing hers. Okay, he'd sort of questioned her ability to do that job, but he was joking. Or, if not joking, he was trying to make a point. He didn't really mean it. He'd just said it.

She said it too. Except they both knew she only said it to get back at him, while he had said it because the thought had entered his head, unprovoked and uninvited. That's why she was angry.

He frowned. The sun had come out again and he loosened the jacket he'd wrapped around himself. That wasn't why she was angry. She wasn't angry just because he'd said it. She wasn't angry just because he'd thought it. She was angry because he was acting on it. He was putting the outcome of his case above the outcome of their relationship.

Or maybe that wasn't it at all.

He stopped and shook his head.

"On your left!" Another cyclist, or maybe the same one on another lap, spooked by Brunelle's sudden stop in the middle of the path, like he might step in front of the oncoming onslaught of lightweight metal and rainbow spandex.

Brunelle looked around and spotted a bench near a tree a few yards ahead. It was empty and in the sunlight. He hurried ahead and grabbed it before anyone else did. It was Seattle, so once seated, he was unlikely to have to share it with anyone. Most locals would walk on in search of another bench rather than have to start a conversation with a stranger.

He sat down and tried to make sense of what had happened and how to get out of it. He felt like he didn't fully understand what Casey was actually feeling, and he didn't know how to find out. He was pretty sure asking her directly wouldn't work, but he was at a loss for what else to try. He remembered one of the former women in his life telling him that women understood so much more than men of what was happening emotionally in any given situation that it was like men saw in black-and-white and women could see the entire spectrum plus infrared, ultraviolet, and maybe even x-rays. He hadn't wanted to believe it at the time, but he had always suspected she was right. That was probably why he'd stopped seeing her after that.

"Dave?" A woman's voice called out from the walking path.

Brunelle looked up to see a woman walking a small dog. She had come to a stop in the middle of the pathway, but no one was yelling. 'On your left!' to her. One look at her explained why. She commanded an aura that declared, wherever she was, it was exactly where she was supposed to be. Brunelle didn't recognize her at first, even though he had just been thinking about her. She was in the same perfect physical shape, but wearing sweats instead of a suit, and she'd cut her shoulder-length red hair into a fiery bob. But he couldn't mistake that one lopsided dimple.

"Robyn?"

Shit. It was Robyn Dunn.

"Wow," Brunelle followed up, and honestly so, "you look great."

Robyn gave him a smile that communicated she knew she looked great and she knew he'd notice.

"Thanks, Dave." She stepped off the path onto the grass, but didn't walk over to the bench. The small brown dog of some breed Brunelle wouldn't have known anyway sniffed at the grass absently, but contentedly. "And you're wearing a suit to the park."

He looked down at himself and had to laugh. "So I am. That should be surprising."

"But it isn't," she finished his thought.

"So, um, how are you doing?" he asked. He didn't really want to talk about him wearing a suit to the park, and he genuinely wanted to know. Although he could guess.

"Great, actually," she answered. "I'm doing great."

Brunelle nodded at the canine in between them. "You

have a dog. I don't remember you being a dog person."

Robyn laughed lightly. "I'm not. But Evan is."

Evan. Of course there was an Evan. She wasn't the type of person who would ever have to go long without an Evan.

She laughed at his expression. She always used to do that. Like she could read his every thought and feeling. She really could see a lot more of the spectrum than him.

"He's a good guy, Dave," she assured him.

"A lawyer?"

"Oh, God no." Robyn chuckled again. "I learned my lesson."

"Twice your age?" Brunelle followed up. "Or almost twice, anyway."

Robyn smiled at him. Warmly. "I learned that lesson, too, Dave. I think we both did."

Brunelle nodded. He really missed her. He didn't think about it much anymore. In fact, he'd almost forgotten it. But he still missed her. He was pretty sure he started missing her the moment he met her.

"How are you, Dave?" she finally asked. "Still wearing suits most of the time, I see. Do you have an Evan?"

Brunelle shrugged. Men could be so stupid. Even after everything they'd been through, how it ended, how it had been doomed from the start, how that was part of it, how great she looked just then, how ridiculous he realized he looked, how she was walking the dog she shared with Evan, he still didn't want to tell her he had a girlfriend, just in case there might be the smallest chance he could score with her one more time.

"I hope so," she encouraged. "You deserve an Evan."

Brunelle managed a lopsided smile. "Casey. Her name is Casey."

"Nice name," Robyn approved. "Lawyer?"

Brunelle laughed. "No. I learned that lesson too." Then he admitted, "She's a cop."

Robyn laughed. "I think you learned the wrong lesson, Dave."

"Probably," he answered. "Likely anyway."

She took a moment, then stepped over to the bench. She didn't sit down, and he didn't stand up. He just looked up at that perfect face of hers as she looked down at his. She smelled a million times better than Katie Sommers ever could.

"You're fucking it up, aren't you?" she knew.

Brunelle dropped his gaze. "I'm trying not to."

"Is that true?" she challenged.

"I don't want to," Brunelle edited.

"Tell her that then," Robyn encouraged.

"Tell her what?" Brunelle questioned.

"How you're feeling," Robyn explained. "Why you're feeling that way. Everything. Don't let her invent things in her head that aren't true. Tell her so she knows the truth."

"Truth," Brunelle scoffed. "I've been having trouble wrapping my hands around that lately. Seems like everyone's lying about something."

"You and I always told each other the truth," Robyn reminded him, "even when we were lying."

Brunelle frowned up at her. "That doesn't make any sense."

"I suppose not," Robyn allowed. "But then neither did we."

Brunelle let those words dissolve painfully into his heart.

Robyn stepped back to the path, her and Evan's dog eager to get walking again.

"It was good to see you, Dave."

"It was good to see you too, Robyn."

And that was the truth.

CHAPTER 30

The night before trial. The last quiet before the din of battle drowned out any thoughts but those of victory and glory.

Or just the last night to try to get some rest before the exhaustion of nine hours performing in front of a jury followed by six hours of preparing for the next day's performance, two hours lying awake worrying about that next performance, and five hours of sleep before waking up barely in time to get to the courthouse in time to start all over again.

Brunelle gazed out his window and took a sip of bourbon. One glass, neat. That had become his night-before-trial ritual. He frowned at the view. He used to have a better view of the city but the city itself had gotten in the way. The pleasant lights of distant skyscrapers were being increasingly blocked by the less pleasant walls of ever nearer skyscrapers. He tried not to be one of those locals who enjoyed sending tourists the wrong way on the freeway, but he couldn't help but have fond memories of a smaller, more intimate Seattle.

Speaking of intimate, and beautiful things he'd lost sight of, he had a phone call he had to make.

He just hoped she'd answer.

She did. "Hi, Dave." He sure did like the sound of her voice.

"I thought I might get voicemail," Brunelle said.

"A couple of days ago you would have," Emory replied. "But it's hard to stay angry. At least for me. My brain just isn't wired to hold grudges."

"Lucky for me," Brunelle observed.

"Lucky for you," Emory agreed. "So, trial tomorrow, huh?"

Brunelle smiled. "You're keeping track."

"My investigation, remember?" Emory said. "Even if I'm not a very good detective."

"It's okay," Brunelle replied. "I'm not a very good prosecutor."

He could hear a light chuckle over the phone. *Whew.*

"You're okay," Emory allowed. "I mean, that's what I've heard."

"Well, don't believe everything you hear."

"Yeah, I guess you're right," Emory responded. "You probably suck."

"That's the spirit." Brunelle ventured a light laugh himself. "But I did have a thought. Or rather, someone gave me a thought. But I like it."

"What's the thought?" Emory asked. She didn't ask who gave it to him. *Double whew.*

"What if everyone is telling the truth?" Brunelle said.

"So, I really am a bad detective, and you really are a bad prosecutor?" Emory said. "I don't think I like that thought nearly as much as you."

"No, not us," Brunelle explained. "The witnesses. What

if Sommers and Crossero are both telling the truth? At least as they see it."

"I don't know, Dave," Emory doubted. "Those two accounts seem pretty irreconcilable."

"Objectively, sure," Brunelle allowed, "but it's possible for two people to both subjectively believe something is true but neither of them be objectively correct."

"So, they're both lying?"

"Not lying," Brunelle said, "just wrong. But also partially right."

"That doesn't make a lot of sense," Emory replied. "How is a jury supposed to only sort of believe a witness?"

"Wanna come over and help me figure it out?" Brunelle invited. "I've got bourbon."

"You always have bourbon."

"Is that a no?"

A pause.

"It's not a no."

"So, it's a yes?" Brunelle pressed his advantage.

There was another, longer pause. Finally, Emory said, "You're moving my car in the morning."

Brunelle smiled. "I would be delighted to. I have to leave early for court anyway."

CHAPTER 31

The first day of trial.

"Are the parties ready in the matter of *The State of Washington versus Matthew Rycroft?*"

Nothing important ever happened on the first day of trial. It was just preliminary housekeeping matters. And to make sure neither side got scared and blinked.

"The State is ready, Your Honor," Brunelle answered Judge Richter's call.

"The defense is ready, Your Honor," West confirmed as well.

And they were off.

First were scheduling conflicts. Brunelle didn't have any. It was literally his job to be in the courthouse every day to try that particular case at that particular time. West had a little more difficulty clearing her calendar completely, as was common for private attorneys, but had managed to clear almost everything off to avoid any significant delays. Judge Richter's calendar posed the biggest problem, actually. He had several matters he 'just had to attend to', and he was the judge, so he blocked out a few half days here and there over the several weeks the trial was expected to last.

Next were the motions *in limine, i.e.,* limiting motions. Those were really just reminders to both sides not to try to elicit evidence which both sides knew was inadmissible. Brunelle couldn't ask Dr. Tockle who he guessed the murderer was. West couldn't ask Chen what he thought about Brunelle's ethics. Just laying the groundwork for a good clean fight. No biting, no kicking, no punching below the belt.

Then it was time to pick the jury. Some cases were filled with sensitive subject matter that might make one or the other attorneys want to avoid potential jurors with certain life experiences. Not this case. Brunelle just needed twelve people who would listen to the evidence and, more importantly, to him.

Over the next few days, they worked through the panel of nearly 100 prospective jurors to winnow it down to the twelve—plus two alternates in case any of those twelve got sick or otherwise couldn't continue—who would actually sit in the jury box and listen to the testimony of the witnesses. And the arguments of counsel. Especially the arguments of counsel.

Brunelle confirmed it was an average panel of average Seattleites. Friendly but not too friendly, and generally uncomfortable with conflict. Not always the best spectators to the adversarial justice system. But trial work was at least half performance, and the maxim 'Know your audience' applied as much to trial attorneys as it did to actors and orators. So, when the jury was finally chosen and sworn in and seated in the jury box, Brunelle was confident in the approach he'd settled on days earlier, with the help of his best bourbon and his best gal.

The preliminaries were done. The jury was empaneled. The litigants were at their tables. And the gallery was, well, not full. The Rycroft brothers had no parents to mourn or support them, and their closest friends were witnesses who were excluded from the courtroom until it was their turn to testify. In the back row, there were a couple of junior prosecutors who had come to watch the old man do an opening statement, and a public defender who was probably killing time before her next hearing. But that was okay. Brunelle's real audience was seated in the jury box.

The room fell silent and the spotlight fell on the prosecutor.

"Ladies and gentlemen of the jury," Judge Richter announced, "please give your attention to Mr. Brunelle, who will deliver the opening statement on behalf of The State of Washington."

CHAPTER 32

Brunelle stood up, nodded to the judge, buttoned his suit coat, and stepped out from behind the prosecutor's table. The courtroom was silent as he made his way into the well and took up a practiced position directly in front of the jury box. He mentally rooted his feet to the floor, lest he start pacing. If he took a step in either direction, it would be intentional, not self-soothing and distracting. He had their attention. He had everyone's attention. His next word would be the first word of the actual trial. The battle would be joined in earnest. It needed to count. It needed to be important. It needed to matter.

"Truth."

He paused to let the word sink in. And maybe to let some of it rub off on him, unconsciously of course, with the jury.

"The truth is the most important thing we have," he continued. "It's the basis for everything else we venture to accomplish. Philosophy seeks the truth. Science tests the truth. And justice requires the truth. You, ladies and gentlemen, require the truth. You have been brought to this place and given an oath to do justice, and at the end of this trial it is you who will be asked to render judgment in this case. What more could you want or need than the truth?"

Brunelle paused again to assess his jurors' faces. He had their attention. More than that, he had their interest.

He took those deliberate steps then. Just three, to his right, a thoughtful hand to his chin, his expression concerned. He stopped and faced the jurors directly again.

"The problem, of course, is that we think truth is absolute," he said. "We think there's an objective truth that exists apart from what anyone might believe the truth actually is. And while that's probably true, it's hard to get to, because we're human beings, and human beings are influenced by their thoughts and emotions. We perceive things differently depending on our backgrounds, our education, whether we had breakfast that morning. If I were to tell you about a conversation I had this morning before court, it might be a completely different story from what the other person in the conversation would tell you. I'd tell you it was a great conversation, full of wit and wisdom. They might tell you they got cornered by that prosecutor guy again and he talked their ear off about the same boring stuff he always talks about."

There wasn't laughter exactly from the jurors—it was a murder trial after all—but there were smiles and nods at his joke.

"So, there's an element of subjectivity when it comes to truth," Brunelle continued, "or at least how we perceive and relate what we think the truth is. There's a parable about six blind men who each touch a different part of an elephant, and each describes it differently. The one who touches the trunk says an elephant is like a snake. The one who touches the leg says an elephant is like a tree. And so on. They're not lying, but they don't have all of the information, so their truth isn't objectively true. It's only when you put all of their stories together—snake, tree, wall, sword, rope, palm leaf—that the actual truth starts to take shape."

Brunelle nodded and took those three steps back to his left to his original starting point. It was calculated. He'd started by talking about the importance of truth, then taken a side journey to explain how truth had some flexibility after all, and then he'd come back to talk about the importance of truth again in what the jurors were about to do.

"It might seem strange to you, or at least unexpected," he continued, "for a prosecutor to call into question the notion of objective truth. After all, it's my job to prove to you beyond a reasonable doubt that the defendant actually, truly committed the crime he's charged with, the crime of murder in the first degree. Shouldn't I be telling you that there is absolute truth, and that the absolute truth is that the defendant is guilty?"

A fair question, and one Brunelle saw reflected on the faces of his audience.

He paused, glanced at Rycroft with a practiced expression just shy of disdain, lest a juror expect better from a prosecutor. Then he looked back to the jurors.

"Well, I am telling you that. There is truth and the truth is that Matthew Rycroft murdered his brother, out of jealousy over his brother stealing his ex-fiancée. But to show you that truth, you're going to have to hear the stories of several different witnesses, none of whom have all the information, and all of whom have personal backgrounds, interests, and biases that cloud their perception and recollection of what they know. Each of them has touched one part of the elephant, and it will be your job, after hearing from all of them, to be able to recognize that their stories complement each other; they don't compete with each other. You don't decide which one to believe then conclude that an elephant is one hundred percent like a tree and one hundred percent not like a snake."

He shook his head thoughtfully. This next bit was the part they were going to love, these conflict-averse Pacific Northwesterners. He was going to give them an out, so they wouldn't need to feel bad about having to call any of the witnesses a liar.

"No, you are the ones who hear all of the stories, and you are the ones who will be able to see the magnificent animal being described, incompletely but truthfully, by each witness. Don't look for how one witness is contradicting the other. Look for how their stories could both be true, could all be true. Individually, the subjective truth to each of them. Collectively, the objective truth to you."

Brunelle took a moment. He'd completed his setup. He'd given them the lens through which he wanted them to view the coming testimony. The natural next part of his presentation would be to preview that evidence for them. Tell them who the witnesses would be and what each of them would say. That would even give him a chance to tell them how they should use that lens he just gave them. And in any other case, that's exactly what he would have done. But he had a problem. And that problem's name was Jimmy Crossero.

Brunelle couldn't call him as a witness in his case-in-chief, and in an opening statement, he was only allowed to mention evidence he expected to actually produce. That meant he couldn't mention Crossero at all. He couldn't even say something like, 'The defense will probably call James Crossero as a witness but here's why you shouldn't believe everything he says', because criminal defendants were presumed innocent and had no obligation to put on any evidence. Rycroft's right to remain silent extended to the trial itself and his decision not only whether to testify or not, but to put on any evidence at all. Suggesting a potential defense case-in-chief would impinge on Rycroft's right not to put on any defense. West would object— probably. She should, anyway. And Richter would be deciding a third motion to dismiss for prosecutorial misconduct. Brunelle thought the third time would probably be the charm for West. Or at least, he wasn't going to risk it.

All of which meant that if Brunelle listed off his witnesses, he couldn't list Crossero. Which meant West would get that a-ha moment she wanted when she stood up in her opening statement and announced the surprise witness named James Crossero who the prosecutor either didn't know about or didn't want you jurors to know about. Either way, it would look bad for Brunelle.

Unless, he had realized, he didn't list any of his witnesses. Then the jury wouldn't enter into the trial thinking Brunelle was already one step behind West.

"You're going to hear from a lot of witnesses in this case," he said, "but I'm not going to list them all off right now. No one reads the cast of characters at the beginning of the play, and I don't want you to get hung up on remembering a bunch of names you've never heard before. You'll remember the witnesses as they enter this courtroom, swear to tell the truth, take the witness stand, and tell you what they know about this case. You will hear from police officers, and forensics experts, and civilians who are connected to the case not because of what they do for a living but because of who they know. And like I said, each of them will bring one chapter of the story to you, but you will be the ones who put those chapters together into a complete novel."

Brunelle took a moment to assess whether any of the jurors had any trouble with not hearing names yet. They didn't seem to. Probably because they didn't know any better. Part of knowing your audience was knowing what they didn't know.

"And what that complete story is going to tell you is this," Brunelle finally got to the facts of the case. "Charles Rycroft was living by himself in an apartment in the South Lake Union District. What us old-timers used to call the Mercer Mess."

There were more than a few other old-timers in the jury box who smiled at Brunelle's reference. It was good to bond with the jurors whenever possible.

"He was murdered in that apartment, stabbed five times in the face, neck, and torso. It was the stab wound to his neck that killed him. A knife blade several inches long severed his carotid artery and he bled to death on his living room floor. And while that alone is terrible and tragic and is the reason we are all here today in this courtroom, it was the other stab wounds that provided the first bit of evidence that would lead to solving the case."

Another pause, just to tease. Brunelle's motive was to make them want to hear what he had to say next. And they did.

"I just told you the stab wound to the neck was caused by a knife blade, but each of the other stab wounds was caused by a different instrument completely. A corkscrew. A fish scaler. Even a combination screwdriver-bottle cap opener."

There were looks of surprise, then comprehension, then disbelief, on the faces of several of the jurors. Brunelle nodded.

"Yes, Charles Rycroft was stabbed five times by different tools of a Swiss Army knife. It would almost be laughable if it weren't so gruesome. Fortunately, it was also unique. Unique enough to lead directly to the murderer, his own brother, Matthew Rycroft."

Brunelle threw another glance at the defendant, seated next to his attorney and dressed in a suit rather than jail garb, lest the jurors know the judge was holding him in jail pending the outcome of the trial. Nothing said 'presumed guilty' quite like pretrial detention.

"Matthew Rycroft worked at P.N.W. Outfitters," Brunelle continued. "In fact, he was a sales associate in outdoor camping supplies, the part of the store where they sell multi-tools like Swiss Army knives. That's where he was when police went to talk to him about his brother, and that's where he was when police asked him if he had an alibi for the night of his brother's murder. And it was there, in the holding room they used for shoplifters, when confronted by that very obvious and very fair question, 'Do you have an alibi?', that the defendant answered, '"No. Not right now. But I'll have one by tomorrow'."

Brunelle paused again to assess the faces of his audience. He was hoping for nods and disapproving glances over at the defendant. There were a few of those, enough to make Brunelle happy, but mostly the jurors wanted to know what came next. Brunelle had laid out means and opportunity. What came next was motive.

"I told you I wasn't going to list off all the witnesses in the case right," he said, "and I'm not. But there is one witness whose name you'll need to know. Her name is Katie Sommers. She was dating Charles Rycroft at the time of his murder. Prior to that she had been dating the defendant, Matthew Rycroft. In fact, they were engaged at one point. Until Katie broke it off and started dating Charlie. Matt found out about it. Of course. They were brothers. But it wasn't as serious with Charlie. In fact, you're going to hear testimony from Ms. Sommers herself that getting back together with Matt was definitely a possibility. Matt could get her back, and Charlie was the only thing in his way."

Classic motive. There was a danger it might come across as clichéd. But clichés happened for a reason, and usually that reason was that they happened to be true.

Brunelle took a moment to steal a look around the courtroom. There was a feeling that good, experienced public speakers got when they knew the audience had heard enough and were ready for the speech to end. Brunelle wasn't sure he was necessarily that good, but he was experienced. He had told them what he needed them to hear. It was time for him to shut up.

"I want to thank you, ladies and gentlemen," he clasped his hands together and gave the slightest of nods to his audience, "for your attention, and I'd like to ask you to give that same attention to the witnesses who will walk into this courtroom over the coming days and weeks to testify in front of you. And if you give that attention to those witnesses, and you keep in mind the things I've told you here today, then I am confident at the end of this trial you will return a verdict of guilty to the crime of murder in the first degree."

There was no applause after a speech in a courtroom, but Brunelle felt like he'd done a good job. Good enough, or so he hoped.

But he wasn't the only one getting paid to talk.

"Now, ladies and gentlemen," Judge Richter boomed as

Brunelle took his seat again, "please give your attention to Ms. West, who will deliver the opening statement on behalf of the defendant."

CHAPTER 33

"Thank you, Your Honor," West said as she stood up. She took a deep breath, then stepped out from behind the defense table and made her way over to the jurors. She didn't seem to have a particular spot in mind; she just sort of stopped, off-center and probably a few inches too far away. Brunelle expected her to pace.

Defense attorneys always had the advantage of listening to the prosecutor before having to say anything. It was undeniably an advantage for Brunelle that he got the first word. He got to frame the case, set expectations of the evidence, and present uninterrupted a coherent narrative of why the defendant was guilty of the crime charged. So, when a defense attorney stood up to deliver their opening statement, they were already sailing upwind. But they also had the opportunity to adjust their argument, to tack.

Brunelle had started his opening statement with the word 'Truth'. West would start hers with the opposite. But the opposite of truth wasn't always lies. Not in a courtroom anyway. Sometimes, in the criminal justice system, the opposite of 'truth' was…

"Evidence."

West nodded at the jurors. "That's right. Evidence. Mr. Brunelle wants to talk about truth. I want to talk about evidence. Because the truth is, it doesn't matter what the truth is."

Brunelle frowned slightly at that choice of words. It was memorable, he supposed, but a bit confusing. The collection of furrowed brows in the jury box confirmed he wasn't the only one who thought so.

She raised an index finger. "Allow me to explain."

Good idea, thought Brunelle. But he also had to admit, he was interested in what she was saying, so she was doing something right.

West pointed to the door to the hallway. "It doesn't matter what the truth is out there," she said, then pointed to the floor in front of her. "What matters is what the evidence is in here."

Brunelle suppressed a nod. She was right, but he didn't need a juror seeing him agree with her.

"Mr. Brunelle spent a lot of time talking about the theory of truth, and good intentions, and magic elephants shaped like walls of snakes."

That wasn't exactly what I said, he thought with a wince.

"But there won't be any elephants, or snakes, or blind men who for some reason are unable to walk around the elephant and touch it all over. What there will be is evidence. Or rather," another index finger to the sky, "evidence is what there won't be."

Brunelle had to hand it to her. She could turn a phrase.

"There's a reason Mr. Brunelle didn't want to list the witnesses you're going to hear from," West continued. "The reason is, the single most important witness in this case is one the State won't be calling to the witness stand. We will. The defense. Mr. Rycroft and me."

Everyone knows who you are. He didn't roll his eyes, but he noticed he was having to suppress a lot of facial expressions so far. Probably another indication of West's success in engaging the audience herself.

"That witness is a man named James Crossero," West had no hesitation naming her witness, "and he is going to come into this hallowed courtroom, raise his right hand to swear to tell the truth, the whole truth, and nothing but the truth, and then he is going to sit on that witness stand right there and tell you that Matthew Rycroft was with him the entire night on the night Matt's brother Charlie was murdered."

Brunelle wasn't worried about his facial expression anymore. He wanted to see how the jurors' faces looked. And he didn't like it. They seemed surprised by that revelation. After all, if it were true, why would he be charged with murder?

Brunelle allowed himself the slightest of smiles. He had been careful not to mention in his opening statement what Katie Sommers was going to say about Matt stealing away to be with her. That meant Katie would be the a-ha witness who undercut Crossero's claim, not the other way around. It was a little like negotiating a price. Whoever made the first offer usually lost, and West just made the first offer.

"Let me say that again," West emphasized. "James Crossero will testify that my client was with him the entire night and therefore could not have been the murderer. That, ladies and gentlemen, is evidence. And that's what you have to base your decision on. Not magical elephants and fantasies that everyone tells the truth."

Brunelle did not understand why she thought the elephant was magical.

"If everyone told the truth, we wouldn't be here," West continued. "We're here because not everyone has told the truth, and perhaps even more importantly, not everyone," a withering glare at Brunelle, "has been willing to believe the truth."

Brunelle maintained his poker face once again. He pretended to take some notes on the legal pad in front of him.

"But you, ladies and gentlemen," West turned back to the jurors, "you will believe the truth. In fact, you've sworn an oath to believe the truth."

Brunelle wasn't sure that was exactly accurate.

"So, when James Crossero takes the stand and tells you Matt Rycroft didn't murder his brother, believe him," West concluded. "And then go back into that jury room and fill out that verdict form with the only verdict that will be supported by actual evidence: not guilty."

West turned on her heel and marched back to the defense table. Her opening statement leaned heavily on Crossero, but then again, so did her case.

And speaking of cases, it was time for Brunelle to start his.

"Mr. Brunelle," Judge Richter looked down at him. "The State may call its first witness."

Brunelle stood up to address the court. "Thank you, Your Honor. The State calls Ramona Gray to the stand."

CHAPTER 34

Brunelle walked to the back of the courtroom to fetch his witness from the hallway. Witnesses weren't allowed to hear each other testify, lest they adjust their testimony to match. That was the same reason they couldn't listen to the lawyers summarize the expected testimony in their opening statements. Gray was unlikely to care enough about anyone involved to bother adjusting what little she did know, but rules were rules and they applied to all of the witnesses equally. So, Gray waited in the hallway until Brunelle opened the door, spotted her sitting on a bench near the door, and motioned for her to come inside.

She was dressed in a simple jacket and skirt, the sort of thing she might wear to a job interview. Brunelle appreciated the effort. She wasn't going to make or break the case, but she would help set a good tone. Appropriately serious.

Brunelle stepped aside to let her through the door then pointed toward the front of the courtroom. "Just walk up to the bench and Judge Richter will swear you in."

"Judge Richter?" Gray chuckled. "Seriously?"

Brunelle didn't understand. "Yeah. That's his name. So

what?"

"It's just that 'Richter' is the German word for 'judge'," Gray explained. "So, it's like his name is Judge Judge. It's just kind of silly."

"You speak German?" Brunelle was surprised. It seemed like that was important for some reason he couldn't immediately remember.

Gray shrugged. "A little. I did a year abroad there in college. It was one of the few things Charlie and I had in common."

"Wait, what?"

"Mr. Brunelle," Judge Judge called out. Everyone was waiting on him. "Your witness may come forward."

Brunelle took a beat then gestured toward the front of the courtroom again. Gray made her way to the bench where Judge Richter did in fact swear her in. She took her seat on the witness stand. And Brunelle began his case-in-chief.

"Please state your name for the record." That was always the first question of every witness. Especially when he hadn't given the jury the names in advance.

"Ramona Gray."

But still just a name. The next thing the jury needed to know was how she was related to the case.

"Did you know Charles Rycroft?"

"Yes, sir, I did." Nice. The formality matched her attire.

"How did you know Charles Rycroft?"

"He was my neighbor," she explained. "Our apartments were next door to each other."

"Would you also say you were friends?" Brunelle probed.

Gray's mouth twisted into a knot and she shrugged. "I

mean, no, not really. We never really hung out or anything. We'd say 'Hi' in the hallway or whatever, but that was pretty much it."

That was good. Gray was probably the only witness without some bias in favor of or against another witness, or the victim.

"Alright then," Brunelle segued, "I'd like to direct your attention to the night you called the police about your neighbor, Charlie Rycroft. Do you remember that night?"

"How could I forget?" It wasn't a joke. Her face was deathly serious. Literally.

"Why did you call the police that night?"

"I'm the one who found him," Gray answered.

"Where?"

"In his apartment."

"What condition was he in?" Brunelle asked.

Gray frowned slightly. "Um, he was dead."

Brunelle took just a moment before he asked his next question. For one thing, he wanted to give the jury an extra moment to linger on the phrase 'he was dead'. For another, the exchange between him and Gray was going quickly, and he didn't want it to turn into an aggressive staccato. She was a good witness for him; he didn't want the jury to think he was grilling her.

"Could you please tell the jury," he continued, "how Charlie looked when you found him and why you concluded he was dead?"

Gray winced at the request, or at least the memory, maybe both, but she turned to the jury box to tell them what she saw that fateful night.

"I walked into his apartment, and—Oh." She looked

back at Brunelle. "Should I say why I went into his apartment?"

"We'll come back to that," Brunelle assured her. "Go ahead and tell us about Charlie first."

Normally he would have kept the presentation of Gray's information perfectly linear. Chronological testimony was always easier for a jury to follow. But he wanted to get the image of the body in front of the jury as quickly as possible. Plus, there was suddenly something bugging him about that misdelivered package story. He wanted to give his brain a chance to sort it out while she talked.

"Okay." Gray turned back to the jurors. "I walked into his apartment, and I didn't see him at first. I called out his name, but there was no response. I thought maybe he had his earbuds in or something, so I walked into the living room and that's when I saw him, lying on the floor."

"Did he appear to be in distress?" Brunelle interjected.

"Oh, yes," Gray answered. "He was lying on his back with his arms out to the side, just staring up at the ceiling with his mouth open. His shirt was all bloody and there was a big pool of blood on the carpet all around him."

"Did you try to help him?" Brunelle asked.

"Like C.P.R. or something?" Gray questioned. "No. I mean, it was pretty obvious he was dead. His eyes were open, but they weren't looking at anything, you know? So, I just ran out again, back to my apartment, and called 9-1-1."

Brunelle nodded. That seemed believable, at least to him. Probably the jury too. Why would she lie?

"Did you wait for the police at your apartment," he asked, "or did you go back to Charlie's?"

Gray shook her head. "I did not go back there. I didn't need to see that again. That was… horrific."

'*Horrific*'. Brunelle liked that word. He might use it in his closing argument.

"Okay, let's circle back to why you were in his apartment in the first place," Brunelle returned to that topic. He wasn't going to end on it. He was going to sandwich between her initial description of the body and having her repeat some part of that description, if only to be able to end his examination on that. "Why did you go inside, and how did you do that? You said you weren't really friends, so you didn't have a key, did you?"

"No, I didn't have a key," Gray agreed. "I was trying to return a package that got misdelivered to me. Well, not return. I was trying to not return it. I mean," she took a deep breath, "a package addressed to him accidentally got delivered to me. I was trying to give it to him."

"Had you been having difficulty doing that?" Brunelle prompted.

"Yes." Gray nodded. "I figured I would run into him, but I kept missing him, I guess. Maybe he was out of town or something, I don't really know. Anyway, that night, I heard someone in the apartment through the wall, so I thought I'd try one more time. That's why I went over."

"Was the door ajar?" Brunelle asked.

"No, but when no one answered my knocking, I tried the handle," Gray admitted. "I was really sick of having that package and I knew someone was home because I heard them."

"What was the package?" Brunelle asked. That's when he realized what was bugging him.

"A bottle of whiskey," Gray answered.

"Canadian Mist, right?" Brunelle asked.

"Right."

"Did you find that interesting at all?" Brunelle asked her, for the first time veering off script, not knowing what the answer to his question would be. "Funny even?"

Gray just frowned. "I mean, it's not the best whiskey, but whatever. It didn't seem funny to me."

Brunelle decided not to pursue it. He was just wondering. But he didn't need the jury to start wondering about things too. It was time to put that other piece of dead-guy-bread on the testimony sandwich.

"Now, you said you heard someone inside the apartment, through your wall, is that correct?"

"Correct."

"Did it sound like a fight or a struggle?" Brunelle asked. "Did you hear raised voices or things being thrown around or broken?"

"No, nothing like that," Gray answered. "Honestly, if I'd heard that, I probably wouldn't have gone over. I'm not looking for other people's drama, you know? I mean, if I heard someone getting hurt, I might call the police or something. But it wasn't anything like that. It just was somebody moving around inside. The walls are pretty thin, I guess."

"Did you see anyone leaving the apartment or running down the hall when you went into the hallway at first?"

"No," Gray said, "but then again, I didn't know I should have been looking. I just wanted to get rid of that package."

"When you went inside," Brunelle continued, "did you notice anyone else in the apartment?"

"I didn't see anyone," Gray answered, "but again, I wasn't looking for anyone. I mean, I was looking for Charlie, but then I found him, and I got out of there as fast as I could."

That made sense. It was believable. A perfect place to

end.

"Thank you, Ms. Gray," said Brunelle. "No further questions."

As he sat down again, Judge Richter nodded down to the defense table. "Any cross-examination, Ms. West?"

West stood up and nodded back to the judge. "Yes, Your Honor. Thank you."

She came out from behind her table and approached the witness stand with noticeably more confidence than she had displayed during her opening statement.

"Good morning, Ms. Gray," she began. "Thank you for being here today."

Gray shrugged awkwardly. "Well, I got a subpoena, you know?"

"From the prosecutor, correct?" West followed up.

"Um, yeah, I think so," Gray answered.

"Because he wanted the jury to hear from you," West added.

"I guess so," Gray went ahead and agreed. "I mean, I'm not really sure how it works."

"How it works, Ms. Gray," West explained, "is that the prosecutor picks and chooses which witnesses he wants the jury to hear from and then only sends subpoenas to the ones he wants."

"Um, okay," Gray said in response. "Is that a question?"

Brunelle stood up. "Objection, Your Honor." He tried to look righteously annoyed but not worried. "It is not a question, and it's not even accurate. It's argumentative and it's uncalled for."

West looked up at the judge to make a reply, but he didn't let her.

"You'll get a chance to make those sorts of arguments in your closing argument, Ms. West," Richter said. "For now, either pose a question tailored to this witness or sit down."

"Yes, Your Honor," she said. "Of course, Your Honor. Thank you, Your Honor."

'Your Honor' was one of those phrases, Brunelle noted, that meant itself less and less the more times it was said.

"Fine. A question for Ms. Gray," West continued, almost to herself. "Ms. Gray?"

"Yes?" Gray answered with some obvious trepidation forming.

"You never intended to return that package to the sender, did you?"

"I mean, I would have eventually," Gray said. "But I was hoping I could give it to Charlie."

"Because you bought that whiskey yourself, didn't you?" West accused. "It was an excuse to manufacture a sort of date and have drinks with Charlie Rycroft, wasn't it?"

Gray's eyebrows knitted together. "Absolutely not."

"Isn't it true, Ms. Gray," West forged ahead, "that there was no way for you to return that bottle of whiskey because there was no return address on the box?"

"Uh," Gray seemed stunned for a moment. "I didn't know that."

"You didn't know that package you were going to return to sender didn't have a sender, Ms. Gray?" West scoffed. "Is that your testimony?"

"I guess I hadn't gotten that far yet," Gray defended.

"Because it was never your intention to return a present to yourself, correct?" West continued to push.

"I didn't buy it myself, ma'am," Gray responded, adding

some force to her voice. "It was misdelivered to me, and I was trying to give it to him."

"Oh, please," West laughed. "Who gives discount whiskey as a gift? Unless there's an inside joke there between two people."

She knows 'Mist' is German for 'shit'? Brunelle was more than a little surprised. He himself had forgotten all about it, to the point that he had barely been able to remember it even when prompted by Gray's comment about Judge Judge the *Richter*.

Gray waited for an actual question she could answer, but there being none, she just shook her head at West. "I'm not sure what you mean."

"What I mean," West huffed, "is that you were going use that bottle of cheap whiskey as an excuse to hit on Charlie that night."

Or maybe West didn't know 'shit' after all. But maybe she had stumbled into something without even realizing it. Was the bottle of Canadian *Mist* actually a threat instead of a gift? A message to Charlie that he was shit? It didn't make sense that it came from Gray; why would she have told the police about it? But then who sent it? Because whoever sent it was probably the killer.

Oh wait, Brunelle caught himself. Matthew Rycroft was the killer. He supposed he should try to remember that.

"Ma'am, I hardly knew him," Gray insisted. "I was just trying to be a good neighbor."

"You were in love with Charlie Rycroft," West insisted, "but he didn't return your affections!"

It was a pretty naked attempt to accuse someone else of having committed the murder. Brunelle supposed that was smart. It might not be enough to argue Matt couldn't have done it if West couldn't also provide an alternate suspect. Brunelle could have objected. West had stopped asking questions and was just spouting her conspiracy theory. But Brunelle knew if he objected, it would look like he was trying to protect Gray, and that would look like there might be some truth to what West was alleging.

He would have to rely on Ramona Gray to handle West herself. Fortunately, Gray was more than up to the challenge.

"No," Gray replied calmly, "that's simply not true. I was not in love with Charlie Rycroft. I barely knew him. We just happened to live next to each other."

"But you listened through your wall to see if he was home so you could go see him," West argued. "You admitted as much just minutes ago."

"I didn't admit anything," Gray replied. "I told you. And I wasn't listening for him. I just heard him. Or maybe I heard your client, after he murdered him."

If jurors were allowed to speak, they would have let loose with a collective, 'Oooooh!'

West was sent stumbling, figuratively of course. She stood her actual ground, but her footing was weak.

"Or maybe you were the killer," West shot back. "Unrequited love is the oldest motive there is."

"Unrequited love is usually a motive for suicide," Gray pointed out. "Ask Ophelia. The oldest murder was supposedly Cain and Abel, right? That motive was jealousy, I think."

Brunelle didn't even try to suppress his smile. He was ecstatic that he hadn't objected to protect Gray. He didn't care if the jury saw his grin. They'd just seen the same beat-down as he had.

West forced her own smile, a thin, hateful smirk. "I think

I've made my point," she non-asked. "No further questions, Your Honor."

Brunelle watched her march back to her counsel table, then Judge Richter asked from on high, "Any cross-examination, Mr. Brunelle?"

Brunelle was happy to stand up and answer, "No, Your Honor." He couldn't do any better than what Gray had just done herself.

The judge excused the witness and Brunelle had only a moment to consider how ridiculous West's line of quasi-questioning was. No one seriously considered Ramona Gray to be a suspect. Still, he then realized, he was thinking about it. Even if just to dispel it, he was thinking about it. And that meant the jurors were too. *Damn it.*

He stole a glance at West and she seemed a lot less concerned about her performance than he thought she should have. She looked satisfied. Almost pleased.

"You may call your next witness," Judge Richter interrupted his thoughts.

Brunelle stood up. "Thank you, Your Honor."

He wanted to go straight to the medical examiner, but he needed to set up that testimony with a few of the cops who arrived first and secured the body. A murder callout was an all-hands-on-deck situation. Every cop in the area descended on the crime scene and found something to do while they waited for the detective to arrive. That meant Brunelle had way more witnesses than he really wanted, but they had to wade through several of them until finally, a few days later, he was able to stand up and announce, "The State calls Dr. Jack Tockle to the stand."

CHAPTER 35

Brunelle fetched Dr. Tockle from the hallway just like Gray and the others between them, but he didn't need to tell the doctor to walk forward and be sworn in. Tockle had testified a time or two over his decades of carving up murder victims. He knew the drill. Brunelle did too.

"Please state your name for the record."

"Jack Tockle." He wasn't wearing the long, white lab coat Brunelle had seen him in at the autopsy, but his worn, ill-fitting polyester blazer somehow communicated he'd much rather be wearing that long, white lab coat.

"How are you employed, sir?"

Tockle turned and delivered his answer to the jurors directly. All the so-called 'professional witnesses' did that. Jurors preferred being addressed to being treated as spectators. It helped them stay engaged, and Brunelle definitely wanted them engaged about what was coming next. "I'm an assistant medical examiner with the King County Medical Examiner's Office."

"So, you're a doctor?"

"I'm a doctor," Tockle confirmed. "I have an M.D. from the University of Michigan from far too many years ago. I did my general residency at Tacoma General and a specialized residency in pathology at Harborview Hospital in Seattle—or Harborview Medical Center or whatever they're calling it these days."

"How long have you been an assistant medical examiner with the King County Medical Examiner's Office?"

"I've been a medical examiner for almost thirty years now," Tockle told the jurors. "My first job after Harborview was as the medical examiner for a small county in central Oregon. I saw some pretty amazing things in those couple of years, I'll tell you. Then I came back up to Seattle when King County had an opening. I've been there ever since."

"You must like it there," Brunelle commented. No reason not to make Tockle even more likeable than his gruff old doctor with the heart of gold schtick already made him.

Tockle chuckled. "Well, it never gets dull. Just when you think you've seen everything, you see, well, this case."

"This case?" Brunelle asked, even though he knew damn well it was that case.

Tockle chuckled again and nodded to the jurors. "Oh, yes. I thought I'd seen it all. Then I saw this case."

"Okay, let's take a minute to get oriented and make the record," Brunelle said. "When you say, 'this case', are you talking about the autopsy of Charles Rycroft?"

"That's correct," Tockle confirmed.

"And did you perform the autopsy yourself personally?" Brunelle needed to establish that for the record, even though it was already pretty obvious.

"Yes, it was me," Tockle answered. "Lucky me."

"Now, before we get into the details of your findings," Brunelle said, "could you explain to the jury the purpose of an autopsy?"

Tockle nodded thoughtfully for a moment and turned to the jurors again. "The word 'autopsy' is Latin for 'look for yourself'. A person who does an autopsy is a forensic pathologist. 'Forensic' means we're looking for evidence, and 'pathology' describes anything that's wrong with the body's systems. So, when I, a forensic pathologist, conduct an autopsy, I am looking for and documenting evidence of damage to the body."

Brunelle thought that answer was a little too scientist and a not enough friendly country doctor.

"You cut open the body to see what killed them," he suggested.

Tockle thought for a moment, then smiled and shrugged. "Yeah, that's pretty much right."

"And when you do that," Brunelle got a little more specific, "what conclusions do you ultimately determine?"

Tockle nodded again and told the jurors, "There are two findings I am trying to make. The first is the means of death, and the second is the manner of death."

"What's the difference?" Brunelle asked for the jurors.

"Means of death is what mechanism actually led to their death," Tockle explained. "Sharp force trauma, blunt force trauma, gunshot wound, things like that. What was it specifically that damaged the body to the extent that it caused death?"

"And what is manner of death?"

"If means of death is the facts of what happened," Tockle explained, "the manner of death is the opinion of why. There are four manners of death: homicide, suicide, accident, and natural causes. Imagine a gunshot wound to the heart. That would be the method of death, but the manner of death could be homicide, suicide, or even accident, depending on who pulled the trigger and why."

"Were you able to determine a manner of death in this case?" Brunelle asked.

"Yes," Tockle told the jury.

"And what was the manner of Charles Rycroft's death?"

"The manner of Charles Rycroft's death," Tockle answered, "was homicide."

Very dramatic. Brunelle knew there was a difference between homicide and murder, but the jurors probably didn't really, and that was fine with him.

"What was the means of death?" Brunelle followed up. That was where the details were.

"The means of Charles Rycroft's death was multiple sharp force trauma," Tockle explained, "to the head, neck, and torso."

"How many sharp force trauma wounds were there?" Brunelle asked.

"Five," Tockle told the jury. "Two to the face, one to the neck, and two to the torso."

"Were you able to determine," Brunelle continued, "which of them came first or which of them were the fatal blows?"

Tockle shook his head slightly. "It's very common to not be able to determine which of several wounds occurred first, especially if they were inflicted in rapid succession. The incisions I made at autopsy would not have bled, for example, because his heart had long since stopped beating. But all of the injuries inflicted at the time of the murder would likely have been while his heart was still beating, no matter what order they occurred in. For example, the wound to the neck severed the victim's carotid artery, but his heart would have kept beating for several minutes after it was severed. In fact, that's how he died. His heart pumped blood out of his neck until too much left his body and his heart went into arrest. So, the other injuries all would have taken place while the heart was still beating, whether before or after the one to the neck."

"That injury to the neck," Brunelle followed up, "was that the one that ultimately caused his death?"

"Yes." Tockle nodded. "The others all would have been insufficiently damaging to cause death, at least that quickly. The ones to the face would have been painful but were extremely survivable. The ones to the torso did not perforate any major organs, but would have caused internal bleeding that could have, in time, led to death if untreated."

"Was there anything else of note regarding the injuries?" Brunelle asked knowingly.

"Of note?" Tockle laughed at the phrasing. "Yes, the wounds were extremely noteworthy."

"How so?" Brunelle gestured toward the jury box for Tockle to deliver his explanation.

Tockle turned to the jurors and confirmed what Brunelle had already told them in his opening statement. "Each of the five wounds was caused by a different tool. And I say tool because they were more tool than weapon. I mean, anything can be a weapon if used properly—or improperly, I suppose. But the things that were stabbed into the victim's body were designed to be tools for other tasks, with the exception of the wound to his throat."

"Why was that one the exception?" Brunelle inquired.

"That was the only one that was a clean incision," Tockle explained. "It was caused by a blade, and a relatively sharp one at that. It was likely new or recently sharpened. There was no tearing or bruising at the edges of the wound."

"What about the others?" Brunelle asked.

"All of the others exhibited bruising and tearing," Tockle answered. "Especially the corkscrew."

"Corkscrew?" Brunelle knew there had been a corkscrew, of course, but it was a perfect setup to ask the question like that. A *corkscrew*?!

"Yes, a corkscrew," Tockle confirmed to the jurors. "The others were harder to tell at first, although that was mostly because it never would have occurred to me what had actually happened. But after I really looked at each wound, I realized they had all been inflicted by different, as I said, tools, and my mind went back to my boyhood days of whittling sticks and opening bottles of root beer with my handy dandy Swiss Army knife."

Brunelle nodded. He thought about adding a 'Wow', but thought that would be too much. Instead, he asked the question at least some of the jurors were probably thinking at that point.

"Were you able to confirm the other injuries were caused by different Swiss Army knife tools, or is it just your best guess?"

Tockle grinned broadly. "Oh, I was able to confirm it."

"How did you do that?"

This was where the loveable old country doctor would turn into what was probably a more accurate description, given his career choices: creepy coroner. After all, who chooses a lifetime of cutting open dead bodies?

"This was the fun part," Tockle told the jurors. "I needed to see if I could replicate the injuries with the tools I suspected had been used. So, first I went out and bought a Swiss Army knife. The big one, with all of the attachments. Nail file, magnifying glass, you name it."

"Then what?" Brunelle wanted to make sure the jury heard as soon as possible that Tockle didn't stab an actual human with any of those handy dandy attachments.

"Well, I could hardly stab a real person, now could I?" Tockle answered. Again, creepy coroner, so it couldn't be completely ruled out until he said so. "Not even a dead body. We can examine them, but we can't add trauma. I don't think the families would appreciate that too much, do you?"

"No," Brunelle agreed. "I wouldn't think so."

"Right. So, the next best thing is pig flesh," Tockle explained.

"Pork?" Brunelle asked.

"I suppose," Tockle allowed, "although I didn't buy it to eat it, so I'm not sure if that makes it pork or not. I bought it to stab with my new Swiss Army knife and then compare the injuries to the ones I observed on the victim in this case."

"And did you do that?"

"I did."

"What were the results?"

"The results," Tockle turned to the jury again, "were definitive. The wounds caused by the corkscrew, fish scaler, and screwdriver-bottle cap opener were essentially identical to those I observed on the victim here."

"Essentially?" Brunelle had to ask. West would, if he didn't.

"There was no bruising at the edges of the wounds,"

Tockle explained. "Bruising happens when blood is released from the veinous system into the tissue itself. That requires a beating heart. There was no heart, beating or otherwise, connected to the side of pork I purchased."

So, it was pork! Brunelle wanted to say. He didn't.

"So, based on that," he asked instead, "were you able to determine which tools inflicted which injuries on Charles Rycroft's body?"

"Yes." Tockle turned again to the jury and informed them, "There were five wounds total. One about an inch below the left eye and another about an inch below that. Those were both caused by what's called a fish scaler. As I said earlier, the one to the neck was caused by a knife blade. There were two to the upper left torso. The one closest to his head was caused by a corkscrew, and the one closer to his feet was caused by the combination screwdriver-bottle cap opener."

"I assume there are different sizes of fish scalers and corkscrews," Brunelle knew he should clarify. "Are you able to testify that the wounds on Charles Rycroft's body were from those tools of the size typical to a Swiss Army knife?"

"I can do better than that," Tockle answered. "I can tell you that they were caused by a P.N.W. Outfitters brand 'Outdoorsman' multi-tool, available online and at all of their retail stores."

Brunelle smiled slightly. "Even their downtown flagship store?"

"Especially their flagship store, I would think," Tockle answered.

That was a nice place to end it, so Brunelle did. "No further questions, Your Honor."

Brunelle returned to his seat as West stood up from hers.

She made her way into the well of the courtroom and approached the witness.

"It sounds like, doctor," she grinned at him, "you're the person to call if my pig ever gets stabbed to death by an indecisive boy scout."

It was meant as a joke, and it wasn't half bad. But it was a murder case. Humor could have a place anywhere, even there, but it needed to be subtler than that. Someone was dead after all. Someone else was looking at losing their life to a prison sentence.

"I, I don't know how to respond to that," Tockle captured the mood of the room. "I'm the guy you call when you want to figure out how someone died."

West seemed to realize she had missed the mark. "Of course, doctor. I didn't mean any offense. I was just admiring your, well, ingenuity, I guess. A pig. How about that? And you said you used a Swiss Army knife you bought from P.N.W. Outfitters? Did Mr. Brunelle ask you to do that, or was it Detective Chen?"

"First of all, I should clarify that it wasn't technically a Swiss Army knife," Tockle replied. "That's a specific brand of knife and I didn't buy that brand. I bought the same type of tool from P.N.W. because they're the biggest outdoor gear store in Seattle. I also have a membership there, so it was five percent off. Mr. Brunelle and Detective Chen had nothing to do with it."

"Nothing to do with it?" West questioned. "My client works for P.N.W. Outfitters. Doesn't that seem like a little too much of a coincidence?"

Tockle grinned slightly. "You said it, not me."

West shook her head in a huff. "I don't mean that the murder weapon is allegedly from where my client works. I mean that the prosecutor and the detective told you to buy a purported murder weapon from where my client works."

"They didn't tell me to do anything," Tockle responded. He turned to the jury again. "No one tells me how to do my job. Certainly not a cop and a lawyer."

Everyone in the courtroom believed that. Even West.

So, she finally got to the question she should have asked in the first place.

"It could have been any multipurpose tool that had those attachments, correct?" she pointed out. "You're not testifying, are you, that you know with any degree of certainty that the weapon in this case was necessarily made or sold by P.N.W. Outfitters?"

Tockle nodded. "Correct, I am not saying that. I am saying the injuries I described were caused by the tools I listed. They could have come from any multi-tool, maybe from P.N.W. Outfitters, maybe Swiss Army, maybe another brand."

"Exactly!" West grinned and jabbed a triumphant finger at the witness. "And so, wouldn't you also agree," she tried to press her advantage, "that Detective Chen jumped to a completely unsupported conclusion when he decided my client was guilty just because of where he worked?"

Brunelle considered objecting. It was well-settled law that one witness couldn't testify that they thought another witness was lying. This wasn't that exactly, but it wasn't too far off either. But objections were for hiding stuff. That was for defense attorneys. If Brunelle had to protect his lead detective from his medical examiner, he was in bigger trouble than he knew.

He kept quiet and let his witness handle the question.

"As I said previously," Tockle responded, "I wouldn't

take medical advice from a detective, and I don't suppose a detective should take investigative advice from anyone as unqualified in that area as me," he took a beat, then added, "or you, counselor."

West lost her smile. Brunelle found his. And Judge Richter covered his mouth with his hand lest the jurors see his reaction.

After a moment, West shook her head at the good doctor.

"Fine," she muttered. Then she posed her last question, probably the only one she should have bothered asking. "You can't say my client was the murderer, or even that his multi-tool, if he even owned one, was the murder weapon, can you, Dr. Tockle?"

Tockle shook his head. "No, ma'am," he agreed. "I cannot."

"Good," West gave back. "No further questions."

Judge Richter removed his hand from his mouth and raised an eyebrow at Brunelle. "Any redirect-examination?"

Brunelle wasn't a big fan of redirect, let alone the way it opened the door to recross, reredirect, rerecross, *et cetera, ad infinitum, ad nauseum*. But West had muddied the waters enough that he wanted to clear them up a bit, at least as it pertained to his own actions. And those of Chen, he supposed.

"Thank you, Your Honor." He stood up and came out from behind his counsel table again.

"Whose idea was it that the wounds might have been caused by different tools on a Swiss Army style knife?" Brunelle asked.

"That was my idea," Tockle answered.

"And whose idea was it to go buy a device like that and

test it out on some pig flesh?"

"That was also my idea," Tockle confirmed.

"And whose idea was it to buy a P.N.W. Outfitters multi-tool?"

"Again, mine."

"Because of the discount?" Brunelle tipped his head slightly to his witness.

Tockle smiled and shrugged. "It wasn't not because of the discount."

"Did any of those ideas come from me or Detective Chen, or anyone else for that matter?"

"Not a one," Tockle told the jurors. "My job puts me in contact with lawyers and cops. That doesn't mean I want them telling me how to do that job."

"Thank you, Doctor," Brunelle nodded to him. "No further questions."

Brunelle returned to his seat and hoped his expression didn't betray how much he was dreading West trying a recross-examination. He hated the tennis match back and forth that could develop when two lawyers fought to ask the last question. Thankfully, West decided to let sleeping dogs lie, or at least let testifying doctors leave.

"No questions based on those questions, Your Honor," she anticipated Judge Richter's question.

The judge seemed annoyed at having his question about recross-examination preempted, but also relieved at her answer. Richter thanked and excused Dr. Tockle, then invited Brunelle to call his next witness. This time Brunelle wouldn't have to wait through a dozen lesser witnesses before calling him.

"The State calls Detective Larry Chen."

CHAPTER 36

Chen marched through the courtroom door Brunelle was holding open for him and straight to the judge to be sworn in. He more than knew the drill. He'd testified more times than Brunelle had given opening statements. The biggest challenge for Chen was going to not seem bored while answering the questions, at least the preliminary ones before Brunelle took him through the actual case.

"Larry Chen."

"Seattle Police Department."

"Detective."

"Homicide Unit."

"Twenty-four years as a police officer. Twenty-one as a detective. Eight in Homicides."

Chen delivered each answer to the jury directly, assuring them of his qualifications and experience. Then Brunelle could move on to the case.

"Were you involved in the investigation of the death of Charles Rycroft?" Brunelle pivoted to the case at bar.

"Yes," Chen confirmed.

"In what capacity?" Brunelle asked.

"I'm the lead detective," Chen told the jurors.

"How did you come to be the lead detective on the case?" The jury was probably wondering, even if the answer would be a little underwhelming.

"It was my turn," Chen explained with a shrug. "The homicide detectives rotate nights we're on call. This homicide happened on one of my nights, so it became my case."

"Could you please explain to the jury," Brunelle gestured slightly toward the jury box, "what actions you took when you got the callout for this case?"

Chen nodded and turned again to his audience. "The call came in about eleven p.m. from dispatch. The reporting party had called 9-1-1 to report finding her next-door neighbor dead, possibly murdered. I was given the location and went directly to the incident address."

"What did you find when you got there?"

"Patrol units were already on scene," Chen recounted. "That's typical. They're already out on patrol and so they are closer and can respond immediately when the call comes in. I need a minute to get dressed and drive over."

"What do the first officers on scene typically do?" Those officers had already testified between Ramona Gray and Dr. Tockle, but it didn't hurt to recap their testimony a bit.

"Their job is to secure the crime scene," Chen answered. "Nothing more. They aren't supposed to touch anything or even really try to document anything. The first officer in will confirm there's a body there and sweep for suspects to make sure it's safe. Then they wait for me."

"And what do you do when you arrive?" Brunelle asked.

"When I arrive, I check in with the patrol officer who's

maintaining the crime scene log," Chen explained. "When the scene is properly secured, there's only one way in or out. Everyone who goes in signs in with the officer maintaining the crime scene log. I did that, then went upstairs to the victim's apartment."

"What did you find when you got there?"

"More patrol officers in the hallway," Chen answered. "Plus, the first of the forensic guys had arrived and were taking photographs inside the apartment."

"Did you go inside the apartment?"

"Yes, of course."

"What did you see inside?"

"The victim was located on the floor of the living room," Chen told the jurors, who all seemed to be listening very intently to the lead detective's story. "I walked through the kitchen to the living room and observed him there, face up, with apparent wounds to his face and chest."

"Did he appear to be dead?"

"He was definitely dead," Chen confirmed. "His eyes were open, but he was dead."

Brunelle nodded. He wondered whether West might object, claiming Chen had insufficient information or medical expertise to draw that conclusion, at least at that moment. It would have been a legally supportable, but nevertheless ridiculous objection. So, he waited a moment to give her the chance to do it. But she didn't take the bait, so he continued.

"Did you personally inspect the body to confirm he was dead?"

"No," Chen admitted.

"Why not?"

"Because I'm not the medical examiner," Chen

answered. "Shortly after I arrived, the tech from the M.E.'s office arrived and was the first to contact the body, after forensics had finished photographing everything from every possible angle. The tech confirmed what was obvious, that the victim was dead. Then they carefully collected the body and prepared it for transport to the Medical Examiner's Office for autopsy the next day."

Brunelle nodded along. Typical homicide scene. "So, as the lead detective, what did you do next?"

"As the lead detective, my job is to identify and apprehend the murderer," Chen told the jurors. "I wouldn't get the autopsy results until the next day, so I did what cops do. I started interviewing witnesses."

"Who was the first witness you interviewed?"

"The reporting party," Chen answered. "Ramona Gray, the victim's next-door neighbor."

"Where did that interview take place?"

"In her apartment," Chen answered, "while forensics and the medical examiner folks took care of the body."

"What did she tell you?" Brunelle asked.

"Objection!" West jumped to her feet. "Calls for hearsay."

Brunelle frowned. West was right. Chen couldn't tell the jury what Gray told him. She had to tell them herself. Luckily, she already had. That was why Brunelle thought maybe West wouldn't object. He didn't really mind that Chen wouldn't be allowed to repeat what Gray had told him. Especially because Chen might recount some detail differently from how Gray had testified. He just knew the jury would think it was weird if he didn't even try.

"Any argument, Mr. Brunelle?" Judge Richter invited,

but they both knew he was going to sustain the objection.

"I'll rephrase the question, Your Honor." Lawyer-talk for 'I concede'. Although, they also both knew he wasn't really conceding, just adjusting.

He looked again to Chen. "Don't tell me what she said, but did she answer your questions and tell you information about the case?"

"Yes." Chen kept the answer short and safe from further objection. Again, not his first testimony rodeo.

"Did you take any action based on what she told you?" Brunelle finished his circumnavigation of Gray's hearsay.

"Not directly," Chen admitted. "We did take into evidence a package addressed to the victim."

"What was in the package?"

"A bottle of whiskey."

"Was there a return address?"

"No."

"Did you check for fingerprints?" The jury would want to know that.

"Not personally, no," Chen answered. "I don't do that. I sent it to the crime lab, but the only usable prints they were able to recover were two of Ms. Gray's on the outside of the box."

"Was that significant to you?"

"Not particularly," Chen said.

"Why not?"

"She handed me the box herself," Chen explained, "and said she had been handling it for several days, trying to give it to Mr. Rycroft because it had been misdelivered."

And part of Gray's statement came in after all. Her story wasn't being offered because it was necessarily true—that was the definition of 'hearsay'—instead, it was being offered to explain why Chen took certain investigative steps, regardless of whether it was true. It wasn't Brunelle's first rodeo either.

"Did you interview anyone else on the scene that night?" Brunelle moved on.

"Nothing in depth," Chen responded. "I tasked two patrol officers to contact the other neighbors to see if anyone else heard anything, but no one did. I also contacted the apartment manager, but she was off-site and didn't have any information to provide."

"What was the next significant step in the investigation?" Brunelle continued. Sometimes being a prosecutor just amounted to asking a cop, 'What happened next?' a few dozen times.

"The next significant steps in the investigation were to contact the next of kin and the autopsy," Chen told the jurors. "Those two things came together when I received the results of the autopsy on my way to contact the defendant, Matthew Rycroft, to advise him of the murder of his brother."

"How did those come together?" As if Brunelle hadn't already told the jury. But still, it wasn't actually evidence unless a witness said it, and wasn't that what West said she wanted? Evidence?

"I was on my way to the defendant's place of work," Chen started to explain.

"Where did he work?" Brunelle interjected.

"P.N.W. Outfitters," Chen answered. "Their flagship store, downtown."

"Thank you. Go on," Brunelle prompted.

"I was on my way to P.N.W. Outfitters when I was advised that Dr. Tockle's preliminary autopsy findings indicated the victim had most likely been stabbed by different attachments of a multipurpose outdoor tool."

"Why was that significant?"

"The defendant worked in the outdoor equipment department," Chen answered, "where they sell multipurpose outdoor tools."

"So," Brunelle anticipated West's argument in order to dispel it, "you were able to conclude the defendant was the murderer solely because he worked where they sold tools that might be similar to whatever was used to kill the victim, correct?"

Chen frowned at Brunelle. "No. That would be ridiculous."

Brunelle was happy to agree. "Of course, it would. So, what happened next?"

"When I contacted the defendant at his work," Chen turned again to the jury, "I asked to speak with him in private."

"In case he became emotional at the news of his brother's murder?" Brunelle suggested.

"No, because he hadn't been eliminated as a suspect—no one had—and I didn't want to be interrupted while I interviewed him."

"Where did you interview him?"

"They had a room in the back where they sometimes detained shoplifters," Chen answered. "So, we went there."

"Was the defendant under arrest or otherwise detained?"

Chen shook his head. "No. Well, not yet anyway. I just wanted a quiet place to talk with him and that was what they had."

"So, were you able to have that conversation with him?"

"I was."

"Did he seem surprised by the news of his brother's murder?"

"Objection!" West jumped to her feet again. "Calls for speculation. Detective Chen can't know what my client was thinking."

Again, Brunelle didn't mind the objection. He was actually expecting Chen to say that Rycroft did seem surprised, and then have to explain it away later in his closing argument. He had only asked because the jury would have expected that information and not asking would have looked like he was hiding something. He was more than happy to avoid Chen telling the jury the defendant was surprised the person he murdered was dead.

"I'll withdraw the question," Brunelle offered before the judge could even ask him his position.

He turned back to Chen. "Why don't we go ahead and get right to it, shall we? Did you ask him whether he had an alibi for the time of his brother's murder?"

"Yes," Chen nodded to the jurors, "I did."

"And what did he say?"

"He said, and I quote, 'No. Not right now. But I'll have one by tomorrow.'"

"I'll have one by tomorrow?" Brunelle repeated.

"Yes."

"He actually said that?"

"He said that."

"And is that why you arrested him for the murder of his brother?"

"That was why I detained him," Chen made the distinction, although the jail cell probably seemed the same to Rycroft, "pending further investigation."

"Did that further investigation lead to additional information connecting the defendant to the murder?"

"It did," Chen confirmed.

"What was the nature of that information?"

"An interview with his ex-fiancée Katherine Sommers."

That was definitely hearsay. There was no way anyone was going to let Chen tell the jury what Sommers told him. But it was also a perfect setup for her, his next and final witness.

"Thank you, Detective Chen. No further questions, Your Honor," Brunelle announced.

Unfortunately, West was going to interrupt his perfectly set up transition by asking Chen a few questions of her own. Richter invited her to cross-examine Chen and she practically ran out from behind her counsel table to confront the detective.

"You arrested my client," she demanded, "because he didn't have an ironclad alibi oven-ready for you when you asked? Wouldn't it have been more suspicious if he did have an alibi ready?"

"I *detained* him because he had a motive, means, and opportunity," Chen responded. "He didn't just not have an alibi ready, he said he would come up with one. Like, in the future, he would craft something. That means he would lie. So, yes, that played into it, as did what Ms. Sommers told me the next day."

Oh, snap, Brunelle thought. Chen was daring her to ask him what she said. If she did, it would come in, despite being hearsay—Brunelle sure as heck wasn't going to object. If she didn't, the jury would think she was afraid of it. Either way was a win. No wonder Brunelle liked Chen so much.

"I don't put much stock in what Ms. Sommers told you that day," West replied in a way that was very much not in the required form of a question. "I wish I were surprised you did.

But then, you wanted to solve your case, didn't you, Detective?"

"I always want to solve my cases," Chen agreed. "That's my job."

"And once you arrest someone, then you've solved it, haven't you?" West asked. "Even if you're wrong?"

"If I'm wrong, I haven't solved it," Chen answered. "I try not to be wrong."

West frowned at him. "Why wasn't Rebecca Gray a suspect?"

"Ramona Gray?" Chen corrected. "She was."

"She was?" West repeated.

"Yes, of course," Chen answered. "Everyone is a suspect until they're eliminated."

"Why was she a suspect?"

Chen cocked his head for a moment. He had just explained it, but he shrugged and provided more detail. "She was the first person directly associated with the dead body. There are definitely cases where the murderer is the one who reports the murder in order to throw off suspicion."

"How do you know that didn't happen here?"

"Because I was able to eliminate her as a suspect."

"How?"

Chen's brow furrowed just a bit, then he nodded toward Matthew Rycroft. "Because your client did it."

Nice, thought Brunelle.

"That's what you think," West accused. But it was another perfect setup.

"Yes," Chen replied. "It is."

West was flustered. Not only was she obviously not particularly experienced as a trial attorney, but Chen was obviously very experienced as a trial witness. She wasn't going to outsmart him. But apparently that wasn't going to stop her from trying.

"But why would that eliminate Ms. Gray as a suspect?" she tried. "Couldn't several people work together to murder someone?"

Chen didn't deliver another rapid-fire zinger. Instead, he took a moment to think about the question, and what it suggested. So did Brunelle.

"Yes," Chen allowed. "That is definitely possible."

West took her small victory and walked back to her seat with an over-the-shoulder announcement of, "No further questions."

Brunelle didn't have any more questions either. Not after that final answer of Chen's. And how it also set up his next witness.

"The State calls Katherine Sommers to the stand."

CHAPTER 37

Brunelle was pretty certain Sommers was wearing the same thing she'd had on when he'd had the terrible idea to go to her apartment by himself that day. She had pulled a jacket over that silken blouse, but otherwise it was the same outfit. He wondered for a moment if she expected him to notice. Then he realized that of course she did.

She made her way to the front of the courtroom to be sworn in, her thick blonde hair falling halfway down her back as she raised her right hand to tell the truth, the whole truth, and nothing but the truth.

Brunelle didn't have such a good feeling about that anymore.

Sommers sat down in the witness stand and Brunelle scanned the courtroom to see if there was any sign of Nick Nicholson. Nope. Either they had parted ways, or Nick had a new business appointment he couldn't miss.

When Brunelle turned back to the witness stand, Sommers locked eyes with him. Her expression was similar to what she'd tried with him at her apartment. But not quite the same. Definitely not the same.

"Please state your name for the record," Brunelle began. It was nice to always have the same question to ease into an examination, whether the witness was friendly or hostile. Or, like then, when he wasn't sure.

"Katherine Sommers," she answered. She was a very confident woman.

"Are you acquainted with either the defendant, Matthew Rycroft," Brunelle moved right to her relationship to the case, "or the victim, Charles Rycroft?"

"Yes. I'm acquainted with both of them."

"How so?"

"Matthew and I were engaged at one time," Sommers turned and told the jury. Brunelle wondered whether she had testified before or just had a natural talent for making people feel important. "And I was dating Charles at the time of his death."

'Murder', Brunelle thought, *but okay.*

"How long were you engaged to Matthew, the defendant?" Brunelle asked.

"Not long," Sommers answered.

Brunelle waited a moment for further details. But none were forthcoming. He decided not to push it just then.

"How long did you date Charles?"

"Not long," Sommers repeated, again with no further explanation.

Brunelle was not liking her vibe. He guessed the jury wasn't either. He wasn't going to win the case with her charm, that much was obvious. But he couldn't win it without her information, so he pressed ahead.

"Shortly before Charles's murder," Brunelle made sure

to use that word, "had you started to see Matthew again?"

Sommers took a moment, then nodded and looked again to the jurors. "Yes."

Brunelle considered asking how long that had been going on, but he knew what her answer would likely be.

"Was Charles aware of that?" Brunelle asked.

Sommers hesitated again, then shrugged. "I'm not sure. I know I hadn't told him."

"Why not?"

Another shrug. "We weren't exclusive. And it wasn't like I was planning on getting engaged again, to either of them. It really wasn't any of their business who else I was seeing."

"Even if they were brothers?"

Sommers tipped her head and smiled at Brunelle. "I don't see what that has to do with anything."

Brunelle kind of felt like it had something to do with something, and he supposed at least a few of the jurors might think so too. Hence the question. But he didn't need to insist on her agreement. He just needed her to say what she told him and Chen and then get her off the stand.

"The night of Charles's murder, did you see Matthew?"

If she said, 'No', he was in a lot of trouble.

"Yes."

Whew.

He just needed to explain why that was significant. Time and place. He'd start with place.

"Could you please advise the jury where you were living then?" Brunelle asked. "Where Charles was living, and where Matthew was living? And please include the cities."

"Okay. I live in an apartment in the Roosevelt neighborhood, in Seattle. Charles was living in an apartment in

South Lake Union, also in Seattle. Matthew worked near Charles, in Seattle, but he was renting a house over in Bellevue. I'm not sure why exactly, to be honest."

Brunelle decided not to pursue his witness's dislike of the suburbs.

"What was the purpose of seeing Matthew that evening?"

Sommer frowned. "Purpose?"

"Why did you meet with him?" Brunelle rephrased his question.

"Oh." Sommers nodded. "To have sex." She turned again to the jurors. "We had sex."

A little jarring, but okay. He had his motive out. Tockle had already given him the means. That left opportunity.

"What time was that?"

"What time did we have sex?" Sommers asked back. Brunelle felt confident she just liked shocking him a little.

Brunelle nodded as professionally as he could. "Yes."

Sommers thought for a few moments, mouth twisted and eyes to the ceiling. "Probably around six or seven. He was on his way home from work and wanted a quickie before his big night of gaming with Jimmy."

Shit.

And there it was.

He'd been played.

Him and Chen and Emory. All of them.

But he was the one standing in front of the jury with his jaw hanging open. Metaphorically, of course. He was too experienced to let the jury see the panic incinerating his stomach from the inside out.

He knew she wasn't going to go back to her original

story that Matthew had been there just before the murder, some four hours later, no matter how much he badgered her about it. In fact, he didn't even want to challenge her on it, lest she appear to win that battle. He could call Chen to testify what she had originally said, now that she changed her story—it wasn't hearsay if you were using to show she was a fucking liar—but the evidence rules required him to lay foundation first. Before Chen could tell the jury what she said before, Brunelle had to give her the chance to admit or deny saying it.

"I do recall saying that," she answered when Brunelle asked her if she hadn't told Detective Chen that Matthew came over closer to 10:30 or 11:00 that night, "but I've had a chance to think about it since then, and I was confused."

That was the best possible answer. For her. Not for him. For him, it was the worst possible answer. There was little point to calling Chen. She'd admitted saying it. Having him confirm that would add nothing.

Brunelle just needed to get Sommers off the stand and rest his case. His only hope was that West didn't adjust her plans for her own case-in-chief.

"Confused," Brunelle repeated with a disbelieving nod. "Okay. No further questions."

He returned to his seat and if he had had any doubts that Katie Sommers had been in on it with the defense from the beginning, they were dispelled when West stood up, grinning ear to ear, and announced, "No questions, Your Honor."

Out with a whimper, instead of a bang.

"Any further witnesses, Mr. Brunelle?" Judge Richter asked after excusing Sommers from the witness stand.

Brunelle watched Sommers walk past the attorneys. Instead of leaving the courtroom like every other witness, she stopped and took a seat in the gallery behind West and Rycroft.

"No, Your Honor," he practically admitted. "The State rests."

CHAPTER 38

Usually, after the State rested its case-in-chief there was a recess of at least a few hours, if not the remainder of the day. It allowed the defense to get in contact with their witnesses to schedule their testimony and generally take a minute to digest the State's evidence and rally the case against it. Also, it was standard for the defense to raise what was known in the criminal law industry as a 'halftime motion'. That was where the defense asked the judge to dismiss the case, arguing that the State had failed to produce sufficient evidence to let the case proceed to the jury. It was basically the same insufficient evidence dismissal motion West had brought before trial, only raised again based on the actual evidence presented rather than the State's promises.

Those types of motions were almost never granted, but they were almost always raised. With Sommers's change in testimony, West would have a strong argument that Brunelle had failed to establish Rycroft had the opportunity to commit the murder, but not until after Crossero took the stand. He was safe, but not for long.

Richter would deny the halftime motion and Brunelle could go home and figure out how to salvage his case. So, he was both stunned and dismayed when, in response to Judge Richter's almost *pro forma* inquiry of West as to whether she would like to adjourn for the day, she responded, "No, Your Honor. The defense calls James Crossero to the stand."

Brunelle watched helplessly as West fetched Crossero from the hallway. He had been waiting outside during Sommers's testimony. Brunelle seriously wondered whether they had driven to the courthouse together.

Crossero was dressed in a blue suit, with a muted red tie. Apart from the attorneys, and Rycroft, he was probably the only person who had worn a suit to court. Even Chen's blazer didn't match his pants. Crossero reached the judge and raised his hand confidently.

"Do you swear or affirm that you will tell the truth, the whole truth, and nothing but the truth?" Richter asked, still obviously a bit surprised they weren't in recess.

"I do," Crossero confirmed. Then he took the witness stand and West began her examination.

"What's your full name, sir?"

"James Alexander Crossero," he answered. His expression was calm, but Brunelle thought he heard the slightest tremor in his voice.

Probably wishful thinking, Brunelle supposed.

"Do you know my client, Matthew Rycroft?" West continued.

"Yes, I do," Crossero answered.

"How do you know him?"

"We're friends," Crossero explained.

"How long have you been friends?" West asked.

Crossero took a moment to consider. "Like four or five years now, I think."

"Do you socialize with Matt?"

"You mean, like, hang out with him?" Crossero clarified. "Yeah, of course. That's what friends do, right?"

"Right," West agreed.

So far, so boring, Brunelle thought. But he knew what was coming.

"Did you socialize with Matt on the night in question?" West asked.

"You mean the night Charlie was killed?" Crossero asked.

"Yes."

"Yes." Crossero nodded. "We hung out. I met him at his place after work and we played video games and drank beer and stuff."

"All night?"

Crossero stuck out a thoughtful lower lip and nodded. "Yeah, pretty much. Sometimes it's fun to just play all night and compete against players from all over the world."

"What time did you start?" West asked. It was probably the most important question of the trial.

Again, Crossero took a moment to consider. "Like around seven, I think? It was after work, I know that. He needed to do something first I guess, then I met him at his place after."

Do something. Brunelle rolled his eyes. *Do someone was more like it.* Then he realized he was buying into their story already too. That meant the jury definitely was.

"How long did you stay?" West followed up.

"Until the next morning," Crossero answered.

"How late in the morning?"

Crossero thought for a moment. "Like eight or nine maybe. Matt had to go to work, so I couldn't sleep in or anything, but we stayed awake until like five, so when I finally fell asleep, I kinda crashed for a few hours."

"And in all that time," West summed it up, "from seven in the evening until nine or ten the next morning, did Matt ever leave the house?"

Crossero sat up a little straighter and set his jaw. "No, ma'am. He did not."

Brunelle expected a 'No further questions' from West. A moment later, he wished he'd gotten it.

"Did you ever tell anyone all of that?" West continued. "That Matt was with you that night and simply could not have committed the murder?"

"Yes, ma'am, I did," Crossero answered.

"Who did you tell?"

"I told you," Crossero said, "the day after Matt was arrested."

"Yes, you did," West responded, probably inappropriately, but Brunelle didn't object. Not yet anyway. "Did you ever tell the police?"

"Yes," Crossero answered. "I was interviewed by a police detective and I told her the same thing."

"Her?" West repeated the word. "So, it wasn't Detective Chen?"

"No, ma'am. She said she was working with another detective, that one you just said."

West nodded. "Interesting."

Not really, Brunelle thought. Or at least not for the reasons West supposed.

Then she turned and gestured at Brunelle. "And did you

ever tell the prosecutor himself that Matt was with you all night and could not have murdered his brother?"

Crap. Brunelle tried to maintain a poker face.

Crossero nodded resolutely. "Yes, I did."

"Please tell the jury about that," West invited.

Crossero hesitated, then turned to the jurors for the first time. "Well, you see, I was leaving work, at P.N.W. Outfitters. Me and Matt both work there. Well, we used to, before he was arrested. Anyway, I was leaving work like a few weeks after Matt was arrested, maybe a month, I'm not sure, but that man over there," he pointed at Brunelle, "he just like ran up to me on the street and started asking me questions about Matt staying at my place that night."

"What kind of questions?" West asked.

"I mean, kinda stupid questions, I thought."

Great. Not even good questions.

"Like, 'Was he really with you all night?'," Crossero expounded. "And, 'He went to the bathroom by himself, didn't he?' and stuff like that. Like arguing that Matt could have left for a while without me noticing or something."

"Was that possible?" West questioned. "Could he have left without you noticing?"

"No way," Crossero shook his head. "Not for that long. It would take like twenty minutes each way and however long it would take to kill someone. So, like an hour, minimum, right? I know he didn't leave for an hour."

West finally got to that phrase that, had it been uttered earlier, would have saved Brunelle the embarrassment of the tale of his streetside interrogation. But it would have prevented the opening he thought he saw in Crossero's last answer.

"Thank you so much, Mr. Crossero," she enthused, even

adding a slight bow of her head. "No further questions, Your Honor."

Judge Richter gazed down at the prosecution table. "Any cross-examination, Mr. Brunelle?"

As if he had any choice.

"Yes, Your Honor. Thank you." He stood up slowly and buttoned his suit coat. He stepped out from behind his counsel table and took a few deliberate steps toward the witness stand. Part of his controlled pace was to look confident. Part of it was to steal a few seconds to decide exactly what to ask.

There were a few different theories about cross-examination. More than a few actually. There were entire seminars devoted to the subject, along with countless professional articles, even full-length books. Most of those resources were used by defense attorneys because they conducted most, if not all of their questioning as cross-examination. Prosecutors, on the other hand, didn't get a lot of practice at it. It was common, even the norm, for defendants to produce no witnesses at trial and rely exclusively on trying to punch holes in the State's case. So, as Brunelle slowly crossed the well of the courtroom to confront Crossero, he was reassuring himself that the best cross-examination, according to all the seminars and articles and books, really was the shortest cross-examination.

Be surgical and sit down.

It seemed counter-intuitive. Time of possession was a thing in trial work too. And lawyers liked to talk, especially in the spotlight, so there was that natural pull to start at the beginning and work all the way through the story again. But that only assured the jury would hear Rycroft's alibi twice. And then there was that unpleasantness outside P.N.W. Outfitters.

Brunelle didn't want to go through that again.

"There is no way," he asked when he got one step too close to Crossero, the optimal position for cross-examination, "that the defendant could have left the house for an hour, is that your testimony?"

"Yes, sir, absolutely," Crossero said. "That is my testimony."

Brunelle nodded. "It was kind of an early birthday party, right? Just you and Matt."

"Yeah," Crossero agreed. "He was gonna hang out with me so I could level up my character."

"You two were friends for years?" Brunelle asked.

"Yes," Crossero confirmed.

Brunelle shook his head. "I can't believe he didn't get you a birthday present."

Crossero waited a moment, then asked, "Was that a question."

Brunelle smiled slightly. "No. In fact, it wasn't." He looked up to the judge. "No further questions."

Sometimes it's the notes you don't play.

Brunelle headed back to his seat at a more normal pace and heard Richter ask West, a bit uncertainly, "Any redirect-examination based on that, Ms. West?"

Redirect was limited to issues raised on cross. He hadn't really raised any. Just confirmed one. There was no redirect-examination to conduct.

"Um, no, Your Honor," West responded. "I guess not."

"May the witness be excused?" Richter asked.

"Yes, Your Honor," West agreed.

Richter told Crossero he was done testifying and that he was free to leave the courtroom. He left the witness stand, but did not in fact leave the courtroom. Instead, he stopped in the gallery and took a seat right next to Sommers.

They definitely drove together, Brunelle decided.

The good news was that the jury saw it too. They were a team. All three of them. Four, if you counted West. Five, if Nicholson was involved, but Brunelle doubted that. He'd just been a very smart choice for Sommers's attorney. A useful idiot.

Judge Richter turned to the jurors. "At this time, ladies and gentlemen, we will be taking a brief recess so that I can consult with the attorneys."

That meant he was going to ask West if the defendant was going to testify. A judge couldn't ask that in front of the jury because if the answer was 'No', it could look like an adverse comment on his right to remain silent. And in most cases, for most defendants, the answer was 'No'.

"I don't believe we need a recess, Your Honor," West interjected. "I'm ready to call my client to the stand."

Richter frowned slightly. No judge likes to be interrupted, even less so in front of a jury. Plus, Brunelle suspected, Richter probably wanted to give West and her client a moment to really consider whether it was wise to put Rycroft on the stand. Sure, every jury wants to hear the defendant say he didn't do it, but it also opened him up to cross-examination by the prosecutor. And she wouldn't be able to control that once it got started.

It was also Brunelle's only hope left. Richter was probably loathe to watch such a miscalculation, at least without subtly counseling against it in his inquiry.

He smiled tightly at West and acknowledged her comment with a nod. "Thank you, Ms. West, but we will go ahead and take a fifteen-minute recess. I think we all could use it. If you still wish to call your client to the stand after that, then we will proceed accordingly."

Fifteen minutes. That wasn't really enough time. Brunelle would have to make it count.

CHAPTER 39

"Come on, come on, pick up." Brunelle paced nervously on the courthouse steps, his cell phone to his ear.

"Emory."

"Casey, thank God," Brunelle exhaled.

"It's nice to hear from you too, Dave," she laughed.

"No time for that," Brunelle said. "I need you and Larry in the courtroom in fifteen minutes." He thought about it. "Fourteen minutes," he corrected. "Thirteen, maybe."

"Thirteen minutes from Bellevue to downtown Seattle?"

"Can you do that?"

"I'm a cop," Emory answered. "Of course, I can do that. What's going on?"

"What's better than not getting caught for murder?" Brunelle asked.

"Not committing murder?" Emory suggested.

"Well, yes," Brunelle allowed, "but no. Getting caught for murder, but then getting acquitted."

"What are you talking about?" Emory asked.

"I'm talking about double jeopardy." Then he realized

something. "Make it twenty-three minutes."

"Twenty-three?" Emory laughed again. "Very specific. Are you sure?"

"Yes. It's ten minutes after Rycroft starts testifying," Brunelle explained. "I don't want you there when he starts."

"Okay, it's your case," Emory agreed. "Twenty-three minutes. Which courtroom?"

"Judge Richter. Fourth floor, east wing, last one on the right."

"You want me to call Larry for you?" Emory offered.

"Oh, that would be great," Brunelle said. "You're the best."

"I know. See you in twenty-three minutes."

Brunelle hung up and took a deep breath.

It was all over but the lying.

CHAPTER 40

Thirteen minutes later, everyone was assembled in the courtroom. Everyone except Emory and Chen, but Brunelle had confidence they would arrive as scheduled.

West and Rycroft sat at the defense table. Sommers and Crossero were seated in the gallery behind them. Brunelle was at the prosecution table. No one was seated behind him, yet. The jurors filed out of the jury room and took their seats in the jury box. Then Judge Richter assumed the bench to a cry of "All rise!"

"Does the defense have any further witnesses, Ms. West?" Richter was giving her one more chance.

She didn't accept it. "Yes, Your Honor." She stood up. "The defense calls Matthew Rycroft to the stand."

Rycroft stood up and West gestured for him to walk forward to the judge to be sworn in. He did so solemnly, dressed in a very nice dark blue suit, raised his right hand, and swore to tell the truth. He sat down in the witness stand and looked attentively at his lawyer, who stepped forward to stand directly in front of him.

"What is your full name, sir?"

"Matthew Rycroft." He delivered his answer right back to his lawyer, no glance at the jury.

"You are the defendant in this case, correct?" West asked, a bit unnecessarily.

"Yes, I am," Rycroft agreed.

"Did you know Charles Rycroft?" West asked.

"Yes."

"How did you know him?"

"He was my brother." Again, everyone already knew all this, but sometimes lawyers had to ask obvious questions just to make the record.

"Do you know James Crossero?" West continued.

"Yes."

"How do you know him?"

"We work together," Rycroft answered. Then he added, "We're friends."

"How long have you been friends?" West asked.

Of course, Rycroft had heard Crossero testify, so he knew to answer, "Four or five years now."

"And do you know Katherine Sommers?"

Again, "Yes."

"How do you know her?"

Rycroft smiled a bit, but it was a pained smile. "It's complicated."

That's an understatement, thought Brunelle.

"Were you engaged at one point?" West led her witness, in clear violation of the evidence rules. Brunelle let it slide. It wasn't like the information wasn't already out there from multiple other sources.

Rycroft nodded. "Yes."

"Did the engagement get broken off?" West continued to lead him. Brunelle considered he might have to object after all.

"It did."

"Did Ms. Sommers start to date your brother?"

"She did."

"And then did the two of you start up again?"

Brunelle finally stood up. "I'm not going to object to how obviously Ms. West has been leading her client up to this point, Your Honor, but I am going to ask that she stop doing it from here forward."

"You are leading the witness, Ms. West," Judge Richter agreed. "Please try to avoid doing so from now on. I will sustain the objection if it's made."

West nodded to the judge. "Understood, Your Honor. I will rephrase." She turned back to her client. "What is the current status of your relationship with Ms. Sommers?"

Rycroft presented that same pained smile. "You'd have to ask her. I learned the first time around, she doesn't do what she doesn't want to do. I tried to be the leader in the relationship. I won't make that mistake again. Not if I want to stay with her, which, obviously, I do."

Very obviously, Brunelle opined to himself.

"Let's go ahead and talk about the night your brother was murdered, shall we?" West transitioned.

"All right," Rycroft agreed.

"Where were you that night?" West asked.

"I was home all night," Rycroft answered. "At the house I rent in Bellevue, which is twelve miles away from Charlie's apartment."

That didn't sound rehearsed at all. Brunelle shook his head slightly at the recitation.

"Now, you said all night," West continued, "but did you go somewhere else first before you went home for the night?"

"Oh, right," Rycroft remembered. "I saw Katie first. Then I went home."

West didn't ask why he stopped by Katie's place first. Katie had already told the jurors. Sex. He went there to have sex.

"Okay, and once you got home," West moved on, "did you leave again that night?"

Rycroft shook his head. "No. I stayed there all night until I left the next morning for work."

"Yes, you went to work," West repeated. "Is that where you were when you learned about your brother's death?"

Murder, Brunelle corrected again in his head.

"Yes," Rycroft answered. "A detective came and told me. Along with the prosecutor right there."

Brunelle gave a small nod of acknowledgement, in case any of the jurors might glance at him momentarily. He could hardly deny it at that point."

"Was it the detective who testified earlier in the case?" West asked. "Detective Chen?"

Rycroft nodded. "Yes. That detective." He raised a hand and pointed at the back of the courtroom. "The one who's walking into the courtroom right now."

Brunelle looked at the clock. It had taken them twenty-two minutes. *Nice.*

Everyone else looked at the back of the courtroom. Brunelle did too after his glance at the clock and watched as both Chen and Emory made their way toward the front of the courtroom, stopping to sit two rows directly behind Brunelle.

West blinked at the unexpected development, but uncertain what to make of it, she pulled herself back to her prepared questions.

"Um, okay, so anyway," she struggled, "you said that you found out your brother was dead—"

Murdered.

"—when Detective Chen came and told you. Was that the same time he arrested you?"

"Well, he testified I was only being detained or something," Rycroft answered, "but it sure felt like I was under arrest."

"I'm sure it did, I'm sure it did," West commiserated. "Were you surprised to learn that your brother had been murdered?"

"Oh, yes. I was very surprised," Rycroft insisted.

"Were you surprised to be considered a suspect?" West followed up. "When he asked you about having an alibi?"

"To be honest, that was even more surprising," Rycroft said. "I couldn't believe he was suggesting I had something to do with my own brother's murder."

"Is that why you didn't have an alibi ready?" West suggested. Led. Spoon-fed.

"That is exactly why I didn't have an alibi ready," Rycroft agreed. "I didn't know I would need one because I didn't do anything wrong."

"So, is that what you meant when you said you would come up with one?" West tried to spin. "That you would be able to explain your whereabouts once you had a moment to calm your mind and think."

"Yes," Rycroft agreed, of course. "That is exactly what I meant."

Brunelle hoped at least some of the jurors were having as much trouble buying Rycroft's story as he was, but a glance at the jurors revealed a jury box full of engaged, but inscrutable faces.

"Were you surprised you were arrested and booked into the jail for your brother's murder?"

"I was very surprised," Rycroft assured.

"Were you surprised you weren't released after Mr. Crossero provided you with an airtight alibi?"

"Yes, very surprised."

"Were you surprised by what Ms. Sommers told the police, or what they thought she told them?"

Rycroft frowned and nodded a bit. "I think they misunderstood her. I guess, that's why they didn't drop the charges. It's all a big misunderstanding."

"I know, Matthew, I know," West consoled.

Brunelle went ahead and let his eyes roll.

"So, I just want to make sure it's absolutely clear for the jury," West said. "On the night your brother was murdered, were you at your home in Bellevue with James Crossero from approximately seven in the evening until approximately eight in the morning the next day?"

Rycroft finally delivered an answer to the jury. "Yes," he told them. "Yes, I was."

"Did you murder your brother, Charles Rycroft?"

"No," he told the jurors. "No, I did not."

West nodded to herself. Something akin to, '*Not a bad job, if I do say so myself*'.

"No further questions, Your Honor," she announced, and returned to her seat.

As she did so, Rycroft started to get up from the witness stand.

Not so fast, Brunelle thought, but it was the judge who

stopped him.

"Please remain seated, Mr. Rycroft," Richter instructed. "The prosecutor may have some questions for you."

'May have'. That might have been funny if the stakes weren't so high.

Even if Brunelle didn't have any questions, he still would have conducted a cross-examination of the defendant. There was nothing else quite as intense as the prosecutor cross-examining the defendant. It was the pinnacle of drama in a criminal trial, and criminal trials were the pinnacle of all trial work. The jury expected fireworks, and even if all you could offer was some shadow puppets, you couldn't leave them without any show at all.

But Brunelle had a show. Whether they were fireworks or not remained to be seen.

"Thank you, Your Honor," Brunelle said, standing up. "I do have a few questions."

'A few'. Almost as funny as *'may have'*.

Brunelle wasn't laughing as he came out from behind his counsel table. He wasn't even smiling as he approached the witness stand. He took up a position two steps too close to Rycroft. The jury wanted confrontation; he'd give them confrontation. Normally he would also stand so he was directly between the defendant and their attorney, in order to block their view and prevent coaching from the defense table. But this time, he adjusted his position slightly to block Rycroft's view, not of West, but of Katie Sommers.

"You did not have an alibi ready when you were first contacted and interviewed by police," he began, "correct?"

"Well, like I said—" Rycroft tried.

"It's a yes or no question, Mr. Rycroft," Brunelle

interrupted. "You did not have an alibi when Detective Chen asked you for one, correct?"

Rycroft frowned. He definitely tried to look to Sommers, but she was blocked by Brunelle's body. He glanced at West and after a moment, he admitted, "Correct."

"Because you didn't know who the cops would contact first, did you?" Brunelle asked next.

Rycroft frowned. "I don't understand."

"Your alibi couldn't have been Ms. Sommers, because no one would believe that, right?" Brunelle continued. "It had to be a third person. Someone like James Crossero."

"It was James Crossero," Rycroft said.

"For you, sure," Brunelle allowed. "But you didn't know for sure if you were supposed to go with that story, were you? That's why you assured Detective Chen you would have an alibi later."

"I was just really nervous," Rycroft insisted.

"So, you were engaged, huh?" Brunelle ignored Rycroft's answer. "That's a pretty big deal, isn't it?"

Rycroft frowned again. Again, he couldn't see his ex-fiancée in the gallery. "I guess so. I mean, yes. Of course. It was a big deal."

"But Ms. Sommers broke it off," Brunelle recounted. "That's an even bigger deal in a way, wouldn't you agree?"

Rycroft shrugged. "It's different. I'm not sure it's bigger."

"It hurt, right?"

Rycroft's frown deepened, but he didn't reply immediately.

"When she broke off the engagement," Brunelle repeated, "that hurt you emotionally, correct?"

He could hardly deny it. Not without obviously being a liar.

"Sure," he admitted. "Of course."

"You still had feelings for her, right?"

"Yes, obviously."

"I mean, if you were going to marry her," Brunelle posited, "that must have meant you loved her, right?"

Rycroft clenched his jaw. "Yes."

"And the reason it hurt when she broke it off," Brunelle carried the questioning to its logical conclusion, "is because you still loved her even then, right?"

Rycroft shrugged. "I suppose so."

"You still loved her after she broke off the engagement, correct?" Brunelle asked again.

"Yes," Rycroft answered, but testily. He craned his neck a bit to try to spy Sommers. Brunelle turned and noted that she had slid to the side a bit, so he adjusted his position to block her again.

"Did you still love her after she started dating your brother?" Brunelle asked.

"I mean, I don't know," Rycroft squirmed. "Like I said, it's complicated."

"Well, you started seeing her again," Brunelle reminded him. "Did you still love her then?"

"It's not that simple," Rycroft tried.

"How about now, Mr. Rycroft?" Brunelle demanded. "Do you love Katie Sommers right now?"

He didn't answer. But his expression betrayed him. He was head over heels for her.

"She's a smart lady, isn't she?" Brunelle admired.

"She is," Rycroft agreed softly.

"Did you read the statement she gave to the police?" Brunelle asked. "The one where she said you came over to her place around ten-thirty that night?"

"It was a misunderstanding," Rycroft tried again.

"You read her statement, correct?" Brunelle reined him back in.

"Yes," Rycroft admitted.

"She was very clear, wasn't she?"

Rycroft shrugged. "I don't know. Maybe. She might have been confused."

"Like you were," Brunelle suggested, "when you were surprised by the police showing up at your work?"

"Yeah," Rycroft agreed. "Like that."

"Except she contacted us, remember?" Brunelle said. "She offered to make that statement. She wasn't surprised. She was prepared, correct?"

Another shrug. "I don't know if she was prepared. I'm not her."

"Why would she lie, Mr. Rycroft?" Brunelle asked.

"She wasn't lying," Rycroft defended. "She just—"

"Has she ever lied to you, Mr. Rycroft?"

Rycroft's brow furrowed.

"She has lied to you, hasn't she, Mr. Rycroft?" Brunelle pressed. "About Charlie at least, right?"

"That was her business," Rycroft replied. "She didn't have to lie to me about that."

"You trust her, don't you, Mr. Rycroft?"

"Yes, I do."

"You would trust her with your life, right?"

"Yes."

"And you trust her with your freedom, don't you?"

Rycroft cocked his head at the question. His face was in a permanent frown by then.

Brunelle didn't need an answer for that last question. He just needed the jury to hear it.

"It was a very good plan," Brunelle said next. "I'm telling you that as someone who does this for a living. It was an excellent plan."

Another failed effort to look to Sommers. He had stopped bothering looking at West. "I'm not sure what you're talking about,"

"How much did she actually explain to you?" Brunelle asked. "And how much did she just ask you to trust her about?"

Rycroft opened his mouth to protest, but Brunelle asked another question before he could.

"Did she tell you that if the jury acquits you, double jeopardy would prevent you from being charged again? You could write a book about how you did it, with diagrams and a recipe for murder cookies in the back, and I couldn't do a damn thing about it. Did she tell you that?"

Rycroft shook his head. "I don't know what—"

"And I could hardly prosecute anyone else for the crime either. I mean, I have to prove the charge beyond a reasonable doubt. If I had already claimed someone else—you—committed the murder, well, that would be a pretty big reasonable doubt for any other defendant I tried to prosecute, wouldn't it?"

"I, I don't know," Rycroft answered. "I'm not a lawyer."

"The best plan," Brunelle continued, "the bulletproof plan was for one of you to get arrested, go to trial, and then win the trial. You just had to trust her enough to go through with it. But you do, don't you, Matt? You trust her with your life. You trust her with your freedom."

Rycroft didn't reply.

Brunelle took half a step closer to the witness stand. He was practically on top of Rycroft. He had asked the jury to imagine a case where everyone was telling the truth. But as it turned out, everyone was lying.

Now it was his turn.

"Do you think you're the last witness?"

Rycroft just cocked his head at Brunelle.

"Do you know I get to put on a rebuttal case?"

Rycroft shook his head. "What's a rebuttal case?"

"A rebuttal case," Brunelle explained, "means you don't get the last word. I do. You saw Detectives Chen and Detective Emory walk in at the beginning of your testimony. Detective Chen is the one who interviewed you and Ms. Sommers. Detective Emory is the one who interviewed your alibi witness, Mr. Crossero."

"Um, okay," Rycroft shrugged.

"So, when you're done testifying, and your lawyer rests your case," Brunelle explained, "they get to testify again and tell the jury about the rest of their investigation."

"The rest of…?"

"Sure. Now that you and Ms. Sommers have confirmed what time you were really together," Brunelle continued, "the detectives will be able to tell them about the rest of the evidence they collected against you."

"What evidence?"

"You know it's not just phones that can be traced, right?" Brunelle asked. "It's anything with a computer. Phones, those fancy phone watches, your car. Even those big key fobs that unlock your car from a hundred feet away. I'm pretty sure you can even track credit cards if you get the right warrants."

Brunelle wasn't sure if that last part was true, but he'd heard some other old people complaining once about getting their credit card information stolen by magic tracking devices or something, so he figured it was possible.

In any event, his litany of possible additional evidence was enough to finally pull West out of her seat.

"Objection!" she called out. "This is all new information to me. I would ask that the jury be excused, Your Honor. I have a motion."

I bet you do, Brunelle thought. The same one she tried right after Crossero called her directly to report his encounter with Brunelle. A motion to dismiss for failure to hand over evidence. The only thing was, there was no additional evidence. Richter got it. And he wasn't about to interrupt a prosecutor's cross-examination of a defendant. He had tickets to the show too.

"Objection overruled," he said. "Your motion is premature, Ms. West. Continue, Mr. Brunelle."

He was glad to.

"You thought we wouldn't have time between Ms. Sommers's testimony and your testimony. That's why you were so eager to hurry up and take the stand. You didn't realize we already knew everything, and we were just waiting for you two to confirm it."

Rycroft just stared at Brunelle, unsure what to say.

"The only real question I have left is this: when you left work that night, with a brand-new multi-tool as a birthday present for your friend Jimmy, but first walked over to Charlie's apartment to tell him you won Katie back, but then found her there with him, and the inevitable argument exploded," Brunelle finally stepped aside and pointed to the love of

Rycroft's life, "who stabbed him in the neck with the multi-tool, you or Katie?"

"Objection!" West shouted.

"Overruled," Richter ruled immediately.

Katie Sommers stood up. "Don't say anything, Matt."

Brunelle stepped back in front of Rycroft. "Too late for that, Matt. You took the stand. Answer the question."

The courtroom was silent for a moment that felt like a lifetime. A lifetime behind bars.

Finally, Rycroft hung his head. "It was me. I did it."

It worked. Lying worked. To get something he couldn't get any other way.

"Katie told you she'd take care of it," Brunelle continued. They weren't questions anymore. "She told you to leave the multi-tool, go get your car, drive to Bellevue, hang out with James all night, and don't say anything to anyone until she told you what to say."

Rycroft didn't raise his head, but he nodded it.

Sommers made a sudden break for the door, but Emory grabbed her by the arms before she even got out of her row.

And Brunelle looked to the jury. They all had more they wanted to know. But the case was over.

"No further questions, Your Honor."

EPILOGUE

"That was one hell of a bluff," Emory admired a few days later, over drinks at their favorite bar.

"I prefer to think of it as an educated guess," Brunelle replied, "but thank you."

"You know Sommers lawyered up when we got her to the station, right?" Emory asked. "She wouldn't even confirm her name."

Brunelle shrugged. "That's okay. Rycroft sang like a canary that accidentally confessed to murder in front of a judge and jury and was looking for any way to get a lighter sentence. He told us everything."

"Even that Canadian Mist angle?" Emory asked. "That's been bugging the hell out of me."

Brunelle laughed. "Even the Canadian Mist angle. He sent it. Charlie spoke some German I guess and told him once that '*Mist*' meant shit. So, he sent it in advance of telling him he was back with Katie as a kind of brag. Like, 'You ain't shit. I'm fucking Katie again'."

"That's lame," Emory judged. "He shouldn't get any

credit for telling you that."

"Agreed," Brunelle laughed. "But he gave up everything else too. Sommers took the multi-tool and sent him away. She stayed behind and made those other weird stab wounds in the body to make it look like a crazy person did it. She left but then came back after she knew Matt had been with Crossero for a few hours and made a bunch of noise so the neighbors would report there was a struggle at ten-thirty instead of six-thirty. It was a pretty solid plan."

"Except using the multi-tool led to P.N.W. Outfitters and Matt," Emory pointed out.

"But that's what made it such a brilliant plan," Brunelle admired. "She made sure we charged him with her first statement, then all but guaranteed his acquittal with her testimony. It meant Matt had an alibi for the time we thought the murder was. And I never did find a way to attack Crossero's testimony."

"That's because he was telling the truth," Emory observed.

"He was the only one," Brunelle said. "Once I realized that, and gave up my fantasy of everyone telling the truth, it was just a matter of coming up with an even bigger lie."

"In open court, as the prosecutor." Emory shook her head. "How admirable."

Brunelle smiled but didn't reply. He raised his glass. "To the truth."

"I'll drink to that." She clinked her glass to Brunelle's.

They both took a drink and then Brunelle set his glass down. "We should move in together."

Emory nearly dropped her own glass. "What? Are you serious?"

"I don't want to lose you," Brunelle confessed. He reached across the table and took her hand. "You keep me honest."

END

THE DAVID BRUNELLE LEGAL THRILLERS
Presumption of Innocence
Tribal Court
By Reason of Insanity
A Prosecutor for the Defense
Substantial Risk
Corpus Delicti
Accomplice Liability
A Lack of Motive
Missing Witness
Diminished Capacity
Devil's Plea Bargain
Homicide in Berlin
Premeditated Intent
Alibi Defense

THE TALON WINTER LEGAL THRILLERS
Winter's Law
Winter's Chance
Winter's Reason
Winter's Justice
Winter's Duty
Winter's Passion

ALSO BY STEPHEN PENNER
Scottish Rite
Blood Rite
Last Rite
Mars Station Alpha
The Godling Club

ABOUT THE AUTHOR

Stephen Penner is an author, artist, and attorney from Seattle.

In addition to writing the *David Brunelle Legal Thriller Series*, he is the author of the *Talon Winter Legal Thrillers*, starring Tacoma criminal defense attorney Talon Winter; the *Maggie Devereaux Paranormal Mysteries*, recounting the exploits of an American graduate student in the magical Highlands of Scotland; and several stand-alone works.

For more information, please visit *www.stephenpenner.com*.

Made in the USA
Columbia, SC
04 May 2022

59935709R00139